Pascal Garnier was born in Paris in 1949. The prize-winning author of more than sixty books, he remains a leading figure in contemporary French literature, in the tradition of Georges Simenon. He died in 2010.

Melanie Florence teaches at the University of Oxford and is a translator from the French.

Praise for Pascal Garnier:

'Horribly funny ... appalling and bracing in equal measure'
John Banville

'Garnier plunges you into a bizarre, overheated world, seething death, writing, fictions and philosophy. He's a trippy, sleazy, sly and classy read.'
A. L. Kennedy

'The final descent into violence is worthy of J. G. Ballard. 4 stars' *The Independent*

'Combines a sense of the surreal with a ruthless wit'
The Observer

'Reminiscent of Joe Orton and the more impish films of Alfred Hitchcock and Claude Chabrol'
Sunday Times

'Tense, strange, disconcerting and slyly funny'
Sunday Times

'A brilliant exercise in grim and gripping irony, it makes you grin as well as wince.'
Sunday Telegraph

'The combination of sudden violence, surreal touches and bone-dry humour have led to Garnier's work being compared with the films of Tarantino and the Coen brothers.'
Sunday Times

Low Heights

Low Heights

Pascal Garnier

Translated from the French by Melanie Florence

Gallic Books
London

A Gallic Book

First published in France as *Les Hauts du Bas* by Zulma
Copyright © Zulma, 2003

English Translation copyright © Gallic Books, 2017
First published in Great Britain in 2017 by
Gallic Books, 59 Ebury Street, London, SW1W 0NZ

A CIP record for this book is available from the British Library
ISBN 978-1-910477-42-7

Typeset in Fournier MT by Gallic Books
Printed in the UK by CPI (CR0 4YY)
2 4 6 8 10 9 7 5 3 1

*The best way to avoid getting lost
is not to know where you are going*
Jean-Jacques Schuhl

'Today's programme is all about stomach ulcers and with us in the studio we have Professor Chotard from …'

Monsieur Lavenant clenched his fist in irritation, as if he were crumpling up an invisible sheet of paper.

'Will you change the station, Thérèse? Or even better, turn the radio off altogether.'

'There.'

The presenter's nasal voice was replaced by the roar of the engine. Monsieur Lavenant tugged at the seat belt, which was digging into his left shoulder.

'In any case, it's ridiculous to try to listen to the radio in these gorges – you know perfectly well it's impossible to pick anything up clearly.'

'It was you who asked me to turn it on, Monsieur.'

'Hmm, well … We weren't in a gorge a minute ago.'

The river Aygues wound its way to the right of the road along the sheer rock. With the non-stop torrential rain of the past few days, its coffee-coloured water carried along dead branches which gathered in the rocky river bends like sets of pick-up sticks. Above the cliffs, birds bounced acrobatically on the taut blue trampoline of the sky. Nature was drying her sorrowful tears of the previous day. The car swerved.

'Look out, Thérèse!'

'That's what I'm doing, Monsieur. There was a big stone in the middle of the road. It's because of the storms.'

'You're driving too fast.'

'A minute ago you were criticising me for going too slowly.'

'A minute ago we were on a straight road. You drive too fast when you shouldn't, and too slowly when you need to accelerate. Anyway, in a car like this!'

'It may be old but it serves me well. And you too.'

'It stinks. It stinks of petrol and wet dog.'

'I've never had a dog.'

'You must have had one in the car then. I may be gaga but I can still recognise the smell of damp dog!'

Thérèse gave up. Whatever he said, whatever he did, the old boy wouldn't succeed in spoiling the good mood she had been in since the moment she woke up. She felt serene, happy with the sort of happiness which hits you out of the blue.

'Why are you smiling?'

'No reason. The weather's fine.'

'The weather's fine … Pah! In the desert it's fine the whole time – d'you think the Bedouin are laughing?'

'I don't know, Monsieur. I've never been there.'

'Well, I have, and believe me, there's no reason to smile. Slow down, Thérèse, we're coming to the tunnel!'

'I know, Monsieur. I know the road.'

'Exactly! That's why accidents happen. You know, you're

confident, and then wham! Vigilance, Thérèse, vigilance, at all times. It only needs a second's lack of concentration … Look there, what did I tell you? English bastard!'

Monsieur Lavenant's voice yelling through the open window was quickly swallowed up in the dark shadow of the tunnel, while the camper van which had almost clipped them disappeared in the rear-view mirror. At the exit, the sun striking a layer of rock made them blink. The geological strata formed swirls, folds of ochre, gold or incandescent white trimmed with the green fur of spindly oak trees, all their roots clinging onto the slightest toehold in the ground. The birth of the world could be read there, its bursts of energy, its hesitations, twists and turns, its centuries-long periods of stagnation and thunderous eruptions. Now and then, perfumed clouds of thyme or lavender wafted in, accompanied by the non-stop chirping of the crickets.

'What about …'

'About?'

'I was going to say something silly, Monsieur.'

'Say it then.'

'What about having a picnic after we've been to the market?'

'That's not silly, that's downright stupid! Have you been drinking, Thérèse? I've heard it all now! Picnic? Do you think you're on holiday or something?'

'I'm sorry, Monsieur.'

'A picnic! And then a little dip in the Aygues, and in the evening maybe a dance, under paper lanterns? You'd be better off looking where you're going. Here, switch the radio on again, we're out of the gorge. I'd rather listen to the world's bad news than your ramblings.'

'Very well, Monsieur.'

The first cherries were barely ripe, yet the market in Nyons was teeming like high summer. Space was limited and they had been forced to park well beyond the Pont Roman, which had, of course, only exacerbated Monsieur Lavenant's bad mood.

'Just look at that! English, Dutch, Germans, Belgians … Do I go and do my shopping in their countries? No! You'd think we were still under the Occupation.'

'I could easily have done the shopping on my own; you didn't have to come.'

'That's right, you'd like me to stay shut up in my hole like a rat. I do still have the right to go out, you know.'

'Why don't you wait for me nice and quietly on the café terrace with your newspaper and a cold drink?'

'That's exactly what I had in mind. But don't dawdle like last time. It doesn't take three hours to buy a kilo of tomatoes. Have you got the list?'

'I have. See you later, Monsieur.'

'And don't let anyone rip you off, we're not tourists.'

Seated at a small table in the shade of a blue-and-white-striped awning, he watched Thérèse go off, basket in hand, and melt into the brightly coloured crowd. As soon as she was out of sight he felt a vague anxiety, a sense of having been abandoned. He shrugged his shoulders and curtly ordered a pastis from the waitress who was bustling among the tables like a frantic insect.

Thérèse allowed herself to be carried along by the wave of passers-by, intoxicated by the infinite variety of colours, scents and sounds, as if at the heart of a giant kaleidoscope. Bodies scantily dressed in the lightest of fabrics rubbed against hers and she experienced the same giddiness as she had at dances in her youth. She desired everything, and everything was there. After the gloomy days counted off like rosary beads in Monsieur Lavenant's joyless house, this was a sort of resurrection and she made the most of it, every pore straining for the tiniest atom of life. She criss-crossed Place du Docteur Bourdongle, enclosed by arcades whose violet shadow suggested stolen kisses, filling her basket with tomatoes, peppers, aubergines, basil, fromage frais, piping-hot bread. She tasted an olive here, a crouton dripping with virgin oil there, a slice of saucisson, a spoonful of honey …

As she made her way back, having come to the end of her shopping list, she stopped short in front of a stall selling hats, dozens and dozens of hats …

GREAT DEALS!
FREE! We will clear your attic, cellar or whole house … 500 F plus paid for German helmets, uniforms, other historical memorabilia, Resistance, militia, US …

PRIV. INDIVID. SEEKS OLD MILITARY objects, from flintlocks
to caplocks, matchlocks, percussion caps, trigger guards,
various barrel bands, even in poor condition …

Monsieur Lavenant pushed his newspaper away and stared
mournfully at his empty pastis glass. In theory he wasn't
allowed more, but since sucking the ice cube, all he could
think of was having another. There was something indecent
about feeling so good and everything in him rebelled at
the idea of calling the waitress again. Yet he was dying to.
He would have to make up his mind before Thérèse came
back. He glanced at his watch but as he didn't know how
long he'd been there, he was none the wiser. The sight of
the crippled hand to which his watch was attached decided
it for him. It was scrawny and hooked, like a bird of prey's
talon, the hand of an Egyptian mummy, of use to him now
only as a paperweight to stop the newspaper from blowing
in the breeze.

'The state I'm in already … Fuck it! I can do what I
want.' Immediately, his right arm shot up and the crow in
a white blouse and black skirt replaced his empty glass with
a new one which he half emptied in order to fool Thérèse,
before becoming engrossed once more in the indescribable
experience of reading the classifieds.

BULTEX SOFA BED, new, yellow. 1300 F.
WIN BIG ON THE HORSES! 70% success rate for our tip with
good odds. WATCH THIS SPACE FOR RELIABLE INFO!

HORSE MANURE TO GIVE AWAY.

TWO THOUSAND-LITRE SEPTIC TANKS.

BRIDAL GOWN, size 38 + veil and tiara. 1000 F.

For a moment he saw it floating before him, a wispy cloud of white muslin. Deep in his wizened heart, something came loose. How long was it since he'd just let go, stretched out on the grass and watched the clouds go by? Years …

'There now, I wasn't too long, was I?' Thérèse's voice jolted him back to reality.

'What have you got on your head?'

'A hat.'

'A hat!'

'Well, you're wearing one.'

'It's different for me. I can't tolerate the sun. My hat is … useful.'

'Well, mine is a hat that I like.'

It was a small straw hat with a wide brim which cast a veil of shadow over her shiny, slightly puffy face. Her violet eyes, the only beautiful thing about her, were sparkling with mischief, almost impudence. Monsieur Lavenant tried unsuccessfully to find something to say to make her lower them, but could only snigger and look away.

'At the end of the day, you're the one wearing it. Now, what have you brought for the picnic?'

'The picnic?'

'Yes, the picnic. Have you lost your wits or something?'

'I thought that …'

'You thought that … You thought … I've changed my mind, that's all. I'm entitled to do that, aren't I?'

'Oh, it doesn't bother me. Quite the reverse; it's such lovely weather. We've got all we need: melon, tomatoes, cheese and an excellent ham.'

Paying for his drinks, he couldn't hide the fact that he'd had two pastis and she raised her eyebrows indulgently.

'Yes, I've drunk two pastis; it won't kill me.'

Monsieur Lavenant decided they should take the Défilé de Trente Pas and look for a place to stop on the way to the Lescou Pass where the air was cooler. The road was very narrow and winding. Thérèse drove carefully, sounding her horn at every bend since it was impossible to see round them. The walls of rock were so close together that it felt like being a bookmark between the pages of an ancient tome exuding a strong smell of mould. It was very impressive but slightly anxiety-provoking. The dense vegetation screened the river below, whose presence was suggested only by a guttural roar, an uninterrupted chant. Neither of them uttered a word until they were out of the gorge, and as one they sighed with relief when the little car came onto the road to the pass. The sun was sounding a fanfare and the clumps of trees were thinning out the higher they climbed. Their stomachs rumbled meaningfully and, quite independently, Thérèse to the left and Monsieur Lavenant to the right, they scoured the horizon for a favourable picnic spot.

'Take that little one on the right! There, right away!'

Having missed it, Thérèse reversed and turned onto the track. It led to a not very attractive ruin without the slightest patch of shade. The view of the valley was magnificent but all they could think of was the Drummond family murders or something else sinister and tragic. Despite the hunger gnawing at them, they turned round. A little further on, a side road led them straight to a farm, out of which shot a large hound, fangs bared, slavering all over its chops and howling blue murder. Once more they had to turn back. Monsieur Lavenant was bright red, his jaw clenched in a silent fury which crept through him like poison.

'Are you trying to make us die of hunger or something? It's just like you to do something like this!'

'You were the one who was set on coming here. You know the area, apparently.'

'It's changed! Everything changes the whole time. How do you expect me to know where we are? Anyway, you drive too fast so obviously we're going to miss the best places. We passed dozens as we came out of the ravine.'

'You wanted to go higher up because of the air.'

'So it's my fault now! Was I the one who had this stupid picnic idea? I loathe picnics. You always end up next to a rubbish tip, being eaten alive by insects, sitting on a pile of stones, with greasy hands and warm drinks – that's if there's not some local halfwit hiding in the bushes waiting to cut your throat during your siesta.'

'Let's go home then.'

'Yes. We *will* go home, we've wasted enough time.'

Each of them had retreated into a palpable sulk when, at the entrance to a hamlet, they noticed a tiny chapel in a hollow, with a small meadow in front of it, shaded by three magnificent lime trees. A stream meandered along the bottom of the field. Thérèse braked and gave Monsieur Lavenant a questioning look.

'We've come this far, we might as well have a go.'

Thérèse parked the car in the shade of one of the big trees. The new-cut grass gave off a smell of hay which mingled with the pollen from the limes. Not one fly, not one mosquito. The serenity of the modest chapel with its lime-washed façade surmounted by a silent bell banished all dark thoughts. It was paradise as conceived by a six-year-old. In spite of all his bad faith Monsieur Lavenant had to give in.

'Take a seat under that tree where it's nice and flat. I'll see to everything.'

The bark of the tree trunk seemed more comfortable than the velvet of his armchair. He put his crippled hand between his thighs, and removed his hat with the other. A breath of wind caressed the skin on the top of his head, ruffling the few hairs which crowned it like swansdown, and then swooped down the open neck of his shirt. In the far distance a cock was crowing, and a dog barked in response. He closed his eyes and opened his mouth, since he had nothing better to do. Little by little the rapid pulsing of blood in his veins slowed to match the peaceful rhythm of the lime tree's sap, which he could feel circulating at his back, from the nape of his neck to his waist. *C'est un trou de verdure qui mousse de rayons …*

He would really have liked to remember the poem ... *C'est un trou de verdure ...*

'There, it's ready!'

Thérèse was smiling, cheeks flushed, hat tilted back, kneeling down, like the little girl she must once have been, proud of her dolls' tea set. In the absence of a plate, the melon slices, ham and cheese were set out on their wrappers. There was even a bottle of rosé, cooling inside a towel she had soaked in the stream.

'If I'd known, I'd have brought glasses, plates and cutlery ...'

Something Monsieur Lavenant hadn't felt since ... maybe the end of the world caught in his throat, prickled his nose and brought deliciously salty water to his eyes.

They made a good meal of the melon, ham, tomatoes and cheese she spread on slices of crusty bread, like canapés, using a small knife she always carried in the glove box. The wine was barely chilled, but they drank half of it straight from the bottle like savages. Monsieur Lavenant got carried away, describing the gourmet meals he'd had in some of the world's top restaurants. Thérèse loved food and he remembered that he used to as well. Then, like a child falling asleep at the table, he stretched out, good arm beneath his head, and promptly began to snore.

Thérèse cleared away the leftovers, put the cork back in the bottle, gathered up the melon skins and the ham and cheese rinds and put them into a plastic bag, scattered the crumbs for the birds and lay down in her turn – but only once she'd given a satisfied glance at her hat. There are days like that.

The day was at its hottest when Monsieur Lavenant opened his eyes. He stretched, yawning like a lion. If his right arm obeyed orders, the left remained stubbornly bent, like an iron hook. He had had this disability for a year now and was relatively used to it but it still astonished him sometimes when he woke up. He lay flat again. The play of sunlight through the lime's foliage marbled his skin blue and gold. If Cécile had still been alive and there next to him, he would probably have made love to her. She would have feigned sleep and put up with it, with a groan. But Cécile had died suddenly of cancer almost ten years ago. He had never accepted being left behind, just as certain blind people will never get used to sightlessness. He had been angry with her and, out of spite, had thrown himself into his business with the merciless efficiency of the most ruthless predator. It wasn't for the money, as he was more than comfortably off, but in order to anaesthetise himself, wear himself out, cause himself pain as others do pleasure, until that evening in September when an episode in a grand Lyon restaurant had forced him to pack it all in. He had felt a rush of hot air to his face, his legs gave way beneath him and his reflection disappeared from the spotless tiles above the urinals. His last thought was of his flies, which he hadn't had time to do up.

After his stay in hospital, and on his doctor's advice, he had decided to leave his apartment and office in Lyon and to move into the house at Rémuzat which had been in his wife's family and where he had set foot only once or twice. That was as good as anywhere else. Since his state of health made nursing care necessary he had recruited Thérèse through a specialist agency. In two months' time this odd couple would have been together for a year and he had no idea how long this might last, the future not being on his agenda any more.

A lime blossom, a tiny helicopter, came to land on his chest. He hadn't drunk much but his mouth was as 'caramelised' as after a heavy night. Propping himself up on one elbow, he downed what was left in the bottle of Evian, which a ray of sun had heated almost to boiling point.

Thérèse was sleeping with her mouth open and her red hair (white in places) plastered to her forehead. Her hat had left a red mark on her skin. A few drops of sweat were visible under her arms. Her dress was rucked up in the brazenness of sleep, exposing soft, white calves lined with blue veins which made him think of certain artisan sausages he had a taste for. She was neither beautiful nor ugly, simply robust. Aside from her professional references he knew nothing about her except that she was Alsatian, from Colmar. It was as if he were seeing her for the first time, seeing her as something more than a medical aid, and it disturbed him. One of Thérèse's knees was marked by a crescent-shaped scar, some childhood accident, a fall from a bicycle perhaps … Without thinking he went to stroke it, but at that moment Thérèse opened one eye and he put his hand down again, turning red.

'I'm sorry, I think I fell asleep …'

She sat up, tugging her dress down over her knees and tidying her hair. A few blades of grass were sticking out of it, like pins. Once again she was smiling. The low neckline of her dress revealed a beige bra strap, more suggestive of a hernia bandage than of sexy underwear.

'Perhaps we ought to be thinking of getting back, it's nearly four o'clock.'

'We ought to, yes.'

'What a lovely place, though ... Imagine, some people actually live here ...'

A quarter of an hour later, the car started bumping gently along the track. Before they came to the road, Monsieur Lavenant met Thérèse's gaze in the rear-view mirror. A tear hung on her eyelashes.

'Thérèse, are you crying?'

She sniffed, wiped the corner of her eye with the back of her hand, and shifted into first gear.

'No, it's nothing, Monsieur.'

'Yes, you are, you're crying. What's wrong?'

'I'm fifty-two today, Monsieur. It's my birthday. Silly, isn't it?'

FOR FARMHOUSE RESTORATION, Apt area, seek couple as caretakers, no family ties, motivated, stable, gd health. M 40–55 gen. builder for outside work, F to look after well-appointed house, no visitors allowed. Furnished accommodation + salary, to start 08/01. Send CV + salary expectations.

ICE-CREAM SELLER WANTED, Male, Ruoms area, for summer season.

The other advertisements disappeared under the salad leaves Thérèse was rinsing. Even if these household tasks – cooking, washing, cleaning – were not high on her list of duties, they were nevertheless the ones she liked best. She had her nursing diploma, of course, but very early on, after two or three years of hospital work, she had chosen to practise her profession in a way that let her move around. Maybe it was the result of her childhood as an orphan, hopping from foster family to hostel as if over stepping stones, until in the end the only place she felt at home was in other people's houses. Twenty-five years of spending weeks, months, even years with her 'clients' had given her a quite remarkable capacity to adapt. A split second in the kitchen and she would know where the vegetable peeler was, what sort of coffee maker they used and whether or not they skimped on cleaning products, or, in the living room, what wasn't to be moved in any circumstances, ornaments, rugs, the way the curtains hung or, in the bedroom, a very specific manner of arranging the pillows, all these little habits which mean that no interior is anything like another, although they may at first sight appear to be identical.

She loved living like a chameleon, an actor, even, absorbing other people's lives to the point that she adopted their smells, their tics, their expressions and their accents, and then, overnight, wiping all that away to begin again elsewhere, as a hermit crab changes shells. Alone in a place of her own, she would have self-destructed within five seconds, vanished into thin air, to be remembered as vaguely as the date of a battle in a history book. It had already happened to her once, between two jobs, and it had left her with the painful apprehension an insomniac feels at nightfall. So she had travelled a lot but only within metropolitan France. Naturally, at the start of her career the idea of joining a humanitarian mission had crossed her mind. Reading *It is Midnight, Dr Schweitzer*, about a fellow Alsatian, had something to do with it. But the far away was really too far and the infinite too much of a prison. She felt freer within stable, well-defined borders. Moreover, for her, exoticism was less a matter of geography than of human nature, and she knew that even if she lived to be a hundred she would never manage to see all of it.

Before Monsieur Lavenant she had only agreed to look after women. It wasn't that she feared for her virtue, she could take care of herself, but, never having attracted the attention of men, she no longer paid them any heed. They had always ignored her, except one drunk, once, at the end of a dance. It had been over with as quickly as you remove a bottle top with your teeth. She hadn't been hurt, physically, but the disappointment she had felt, lying on a bale of straw with the man vomiting at her back, had extinguished her most ardent dreams for good.

And so she had spent her whole life among women, usually widows and a few elderly spinsters, from the sweetest to the most cantankerous. Many of them had died in her arms.

If she had accepted the job at Monsieur Lavenant's it was because, although she felt much more vigorous than many a man in his fifties, her age was becoming a handicap, as if old age demanded that its final moments be attended by a grace which she cruelly lacked. At all events, Thérèse was no longer really concerned about human gender, male or female. In her eyes they all belonged to the same company of the infirm, of angels almost.

Nonetheless she was a little discomfited on meeting Monsieur Lavenant for the first time. Instead of the doddering old man described to her by the agency, she found herself confronted by a good-looking, upright man, one with a crippled arm it was true, but tall, slim and elegant. In spite of his coldness and peremptory tone she had immediately perceived his weak spot, a secret wound inside, where he had taken refuge like a hunted animal. She had accepted the conditions of the contract – modest salary, remote house in a small village in the Provencal Drôme region, almost no days off – and recalled how he had seemed surprised, even disappointed at not having to wrangle with her, certainly hoping for a refusal. That had been in Lyon, in a cold, austere panelled office, one, however, which he visibly had no desire to leave.

Since they had been sharing this house, no more cheerful than the Lyon office, he had done all he could to make himself disagreeable, but the more he persisted in this attitude, the more Thérèse took a malicious pleasure in receiving the blows with the unshakable indifference of a padded wall. This was neither sadism nor masochism on her part; she was simply convinced that one of these days she would succeed in bringing him out of his hole. Thérèse was as pugnacious as a pike fisherman and this was a catch she was not going to let go. Yesterday after the picnic she had scored a point.

Thérèse took a salad shaker out of the cupboard, one of those previously used for collecting snails, made out of woven metal wire. Everything was old here, a family house where nothing had been changed except for the washing machine and central heating. She heaped the leaves in the shaker and went to drain them on the doorstep. The drops raining from the salad made dark galaxies on the already warm stone flags. Above the Rocher du Caire, whose outline resembling an Indian chief was silhouetted against the washed-out sky, a dozen wild vultures were circling before swooping down further into the valley. Shepherds must have put out a ewe's carcass for them. She came back to the sink, put the fresh curly lettuce leaves into a salad bowl and, before starting on anything else, touched her earrings with a smile, two little green stones which a blushing Monsieur Lavenant had given her for her birthday the evening before.

Monsieur Lavenant drank the lukewarm dregs of his bowl of coffee, used the side of his hand to sweep the scattered breadcrumbs into a little heap on the table, and then gazed at it. The noise of the motorised cultivator starting up came in through the open window and made him jump. He hurried to close it, railing against his idiot of a neighbour. The farting noises from the countless pieces of machinery the man used every day of the week, including Sunday, were becoming intolerable. People in the country spend their time in strange ways. They dig holes, fill in others, put up walls made of very heavy stones, lug enormous beams about in order to build the frames of sizeable buildings which they never finish, divert watercourses, sand, saw, twist and untwist pieces of scrap metal, cut down trees, knock in posts, heap their gardens with the carcasses of old Renault 4s, sometimes turning them into henhouses, with the result that their properties look like rubbish tips, breakers' yards. The more arduous and risky the work, the happier they are. They can't stop wearing themselves out, baking their skin in the sun, as if the way to save their souls is by the total exhaustion of their bodies. Everything they build is ugly, as are the materials they use:

corrugated iron, asbestos cement, plastic sheeting, old tyres. They don't give a stuff about the birdsong or the sunsets. Nature, for them, is merely a source of income from which they scarcely profit. All this was going to end badly. One day Monsieur Lavenant was going to kill his neighbour.

This murderous prospect livened him up. He had slept badly and since waking had felt listless, caught up in an uncharacteristic melancholy. One half of him resisted this mood but the other would gladly have given in to it, like his whim of the evening before. What had got into him that he had given Cécile's earrings to Thérèse? Two little emeralds set in gold, which he had brought back from Bangkok for her in … Just like in films, to symbolise the passing of time, he saw the pages of a calendar flying off, but couldn't keep hold of a single one. They lay scattered in his memory, just so many days he had passed by without noticing. The feeling of emptiness made him suddenly dizzy and he had to sit down in his armchair, almost winded. 'Bloody hell! I *know* I've been to Bangkok! I'd swear it on my life.' Not that that was much of a guarantee any more. The more he tried to bolster himself with his memories, the more they dissolved into a pallid watercolour, drained of all significance. 'Silom Road, Chao Phraya River, Sathon Tai Road …' Names, just names, which in being spoken were stripped of their meaning and only increased his doubt. He gave up on Thailand to concentrate on more elementary things. Once he had recited all his times tables he felt a degree of reassurance. His doctor had warned him about possible temporary after-effects of the stroke which should, however, not cause him alarm. It must be one of those.

Right, he had given Cécile's earrings to Thérèse because ... because he had felt sorry for her with her fifty-two years and her little straw hat, that was it, he'd felt sorry. And yet, deep down, he didn't think that was the right word. Unless ... unless it was himself he'd felt sorry for. Never had he been so acutely aware of the immense solitude in which he'd been steeped for years as he had yesterday outside the little chapel, beneath the lime tree. Without Thérèse there he might perhaps have died of it. By giving her this modest jewellery he had wanted to thank her, it was as silly as that. But how had she construed his gesture? As a cheap come-on? A weakness on his part? And why had he insisted on grilling the chops in the fireplace, preparing the fire himself with his one hand, opening a bottle of champagne and talking nonsense about his life and his travels ... He was drunk, that was it. He was drunk and had let himself get swept up in the stupidest sentimentalities. Until they'd parted, almost reluctantly, in front of the dying fire. He'd all but kissed her before going up to bed. He was angry with himself now, yes, he was angry all right! That morning he'd done everything he could to avoid her, just a grumpy 'good morning' before having his breakfast. He hadn't looked at her but was sure she was smiling as she brought his coffee.

Closed window notwithstanding, the vroom of the motor grated on his nerves like a dentist's drill. He'd go and give him a piece of his mind, that moron! Couldn't you even have peace and quiet on a Sunday? But was it in fact Sunday?

'You shouldn't have lost your temper like that. It's not good for you and it achieves nothing.'

'Nothing? Can you still hear it? No, well, you see!'

'At this time he'll be having his lunch, like us.'

'That's something. Sometimes those louts forget to eat. Have you tipped the saltcellar into the salad or something?'

Monsieur Lavenant pushed his plate away, pulling a face. He was pale, and his right hand shook as he wiped his lips with his napkin. It wouldn't have taken much for him to burst into tears. He wasn't hungry. The altercation with his neighbour had spoilt his appetite. Naturally he hadn't been slow to tell him what was what, but the other man had retorted that, for one thing, he was at liberty to do what he liked in his own home and, for another, it wasn't Sunday but Wednesday and, during the week, not having the luxury of twiddling his thumbs like some people, he had every right to work.

Stuck on the other side of the low stone wall, Monsieur Lavenant had felt betrayed. He stood stock-still, open-mouthed, until the hulk disappeared, pushing a wheelbarrow filled with rubble. It wasn't Sunday ... Time no longer belonged to him and he no longer belonged to time. A stream of bewildered protestations wedged in his throat like dead branches in the river Aygues in spate. He put his hand to his forehead, closing his eyes. A word was blinking in his head like a hazard light: SENILE. His knees started trembling as they had in front of the urinals just before his stroke. He went back up the steps to his house holding onto the rail, as stiff as a wooden puppet.

'Why didn't you tell me it wasn't Sunday?'

'Well, you never asked me. We went to the market yesterday, that's always a Tuesday.'

'Tuesday ...'

Thérèse saw his expression darken, begin to turn nasty. Embarrassed, she got up and began clearing the table.

'Tuesday, Wednesday, Sunday, what does it matter? One day's as good as another. It's true my salad was too salty.'

Monsieur Lavenant had his coffee in the sitting room. The closed shutters cast stripes of light and shade around the room. The house suited him well, really; the internal walls were plastered and the sun was kept out. But the house, at least, had a memory. He grabbed the remote control and began playing with the buttons the way others play Russian roulette. Except that in this case there was a bullet in every chamber of the barrel. Each of the advertisements streaming by seemed to be addressed specially to him by some diabolical means: Norwich Union, life assurance, home lifts, denture fixative, and featured actors he remembered when they were young and famous. This distressing *danse macabre* persisted after he had switched off the TV. On the convex screen was a reflection of his own image, a desiccated mummy huddled in an armchair streaked with light like an old negative. This was the last thing he saw before letting his chin drop onto his chest, overcome by a pitiless fatigue.

He woke up in the grip of a strong sensation, somewhere between pleasure and pain. He had the most enormous erection. A dark stain formed a sort of island shape on his left thigh.

'What the f—'

He stood up, legs apart like a child caught wetting his pants. It was the first time this had happened to him. Red-faced, he made a rush for the bathroom. On the stairs he ran into Thérèse, who was forced to press herself against the wall to let him go past.

'What's the matter?'

'Nothing, absolutely nothing.'

Bolting the door, he took off his trousers, switched on the hot tap and looked for the nail brush. With only one hand and in his febrile state, every action became hazardous. As he was preparing to scrub the fabric, he realised he was dealing not with urine but with sperm. A readily identifiable thin white film was drying on the borders of the stain. He had to sit down on the edge of the bath tub, torn between pride that he still had it in him and shame at having lost control. The touch of the icy enamel beneath his thighs made his hairs stand on end and again his penis grew hard.

'I've got an erection, for …! An erection and I'm ejaculating …'

It was as though an old piston were starting up again inside his head. What had got this old locomotive of a body going? What could he have been dreaming about?

'Monsieur, are you all right?'

'Fine, Thérèse. I've overheated, just need a shower.'

He ran it over his skin and found himself amazingly reinvigorated, as if the water gushing from the shower head were coming straight from the spring at Lourdes. While drying himself, he observed his body in the mirror. There were folds of skin on the bones of course, but he was still svelte and stood tall. He shrugged his shoulders at so much vanity, but flashed himself a smile anyway, before rolling his trousers and underpants into a ball in the laundry basket.

While he was in his room getting changed, he asked himself the name of the little prostitute in Bangkok, the one he'd found so exciting. Natcharee! Every prostitute in Bangkok was called Natcharee. Maybe he'd been dreaming about her. Either way, it tended to prove that his memory was as intact as his sexual potency, and that was all that mattered. The monotony of a life lived on the margins of the world and its realities explained his earlier confusion over dates. He wouldn't let himself be fooled again. The air flooding in through the open window of his room was scented with lavender and thyme. Above the Rocher du Caire a pair of vultures were majestically following the twists and turns of the rising warm air currents.

'Thérèse, what are you doing?'

'I was about to put a wash on.'

'Can't you put it off till later? What about going to watch the vultures at the Rocher?'

'But … Of course, I'd love to.'

'Why are you looking at me like that?'

'You're wearing your Sunday clothes.'

Once past the village of May, sitting atop a rocky peak, the road wound like a skein of wool between the cherry trees, their branches bowing under the weight of fruit. Monsieur Lavenant made Thérèse stop so he could pick some, which he presented to her with the same smile as for the earrings the evening before. The cherries were crammed with black sunshine and one of them, bursting between Thérèse's teeth, made three red spots on her top.

They had to leave the car a good fifteen minutes from the bird-watching spot. An official sign indicated the point beyond which the track was accessible only in a 4 x 4. They set off on foot, wearing hats to protect them from the sun, which was on home territory here. Other than the occasional tumbledown sheep fold and two or three stunted oak trees there was nowhere to seek shade. Monsieur Lavenant was wearing his binoculars round his neck and Thérèse had a bottle of Evian in her bag. The fields of lavender were crackling with insects. Several hundred metres beyond the point where the pair had set off at a marching pace, Monsieur Lavenant stopped. Large beads of sweat were forming on his forehead and there was a certain stiffness in his foot arch.

The immensity of the sky seemed insufficient to fill the void which was making his lungs wheeze like a rusty accordion. Thérèse was already far ahead, driven by the pugnacity which never left her, no matter what she was doing. She turned round to see him sitting on a stone trying to get his breath back.

'All right?'

He nodded a 'yes' as no sound would come out of his parched lips. He took a few deep breaths of the burning air, bit the inside of his cheeks and then set off again. Thérèse had disappeared from sight now and for a split second he told himself he would never see her again, which made him speed up. He found her, bright red and out of breath, at the foot of the large wooden cross which dominated the cliff top. In a single gulp he drank half the bottle of water she held out to him.

The raptors nested on the cliff face, so that from where they were sitting at the edge of the rock they could watch them take off a few metres below their feet. They were impressive creatures, weighing nearly ten kilos and with a wing span of almost three metres. As their weight meant they couldn't propel themselves by flapping their wings, they would dive into the void with their wings almost still, and a few seconds later were only a tiny dark speck on the other side of the valley. Sometimes one of them flew so close above their heads that they could hear the wind whistling in its feathers. Since they ate only dead things, they were completely harmless, but their intimidating appearance – hooked beaks, fierce eyes and powerful talons – had led them to be hunted to extinction. Five or six years previously, a few pairs had been reintroduced to Les Baronnies massif. Some had readapted, others had not. The day after their release into the wild, one had been found on the roof of the baker's van, and another on the back of a bench in the square at Rémuzat. But many had recovered the memory of their wings and today there were a good thirty of them. The dead ewes that shepherds left out for them more than supplied their needs. With the ability to spot a carcass at more than three thousand metres, they would swoop down on it, and a quarter of an hour later there would be only a pile of bones.

Thérèse and Monsieur Lavenant were 'oohing' and 'aahing', squabbling over the binoculars like a couple of children watching the graceful acrobatics of kites. How heavy, awkward and clumsy they felt next to these soaring creatures, the secret of whose aerial grace resided in their obliviousness of their bodies.

As the sun grew lower, they heard distinct sounds rising from the valley floor – a dog barking, a moped engine, a child's laugh – but it was impossible to pinpoint where they came from. They were seeing what the gods see, which is to say, nothing in particular. Thérèse shivered with the ancient fear which grips humans' hearts at the end of the day.

'Perhaps we ought to be thinking about getting back?'

Monsieur Lavenant didn't reply immediately. His profile was not unlike that of the wild vultures. He waved his hand as if brushing away a fly, and agreed, getting to his feet. A sudden gust made them teeter as they stood upright again, and Thérèse's hat almost blew away. On the way back, which seemed unbelievably short compared to the outward path, they neither spoke nor looked at each other. Only their shadows, out in front, seemed to fall into step occasionally.

'I really wonder why I make dessert for you, you never eat any of it. Strawberries like that, it's a waste!'

It was such a simple phrase, perfectly ordinary, and yet so full of affection that Monsieur Lavenant gave a faint smile. In his head the huge birds he'd been watching still soared. They'd had dinner outside, in the patch of garden bordering the path to the little wood. It was balmy. Pipistrelles flitted among the branches so quickly that their presence was detectable only from the merest vibration in the air, heavy with the scent of the limes. Monsieur Lavenant was smoking a cigarette, savouring each puff as if it were his last. Strictly speaking, aside from the picnic, the row with his neighbour, the wet patch on his trousers and the vultures in flight, you couldn't say that anything out of the ordinary had happened in these past two days, and yet Monsieur Lavenant felt intensely alive, intoxicated by the sweet weariness of days lived to the full. Every detail took on its own particular significance; nothing was without some use – though what this new way of interpreting the everyday really meant, he could not say. He felt as if he'd come home after a long, long journey. It was like reading a book he'd had as a child, seeing an old film again, the subtle pleasure of conjugating the past in the present. Was it important to remember everything? The memory's capacity to absorb has its limits and one day you have to become selective. 'FREE! We will clear your attic, cellar or whole house …' Who hadn't dreamed of one day clearing the decks, of disappearing one fine morning or one filthy night with no baggage but the skin on his bones and the miserable handful of memories that hold it all together? Did he need all that junk one accumulates on the pretext that 'it might come in useful some day' and which, over time, rusts like so many saucepans? What should he keep from a day like today? The crash of the Tokyo stock market or the vultures' imperturbable flight? The answer was obvious.

The crunching of footsteps on the path made him jump. Two shapes appeared at the edge of the little wood, their pale garments creating an aura against the background of blue shadow. A short stout woman of indeterminate age, with eyes inordinately magnified by a pair of glasses with lenses as thick as jam jars, was approaching, holding by the hand a strange creature, a sort of human fingerling of a phosphorescent pallor, probably albino, who could nevertheless be identified as female by the dress she was wearing, which was made from the same beige and blue-sprigged fabric as the short lady's.

'Good evening, Monsieur.'

'Good evening.'

'What a beautiful evening, don't you think?'

'Very.'

The lady's face was unbelievably elastic. The smile she

41

gave Monsieur Lavenant, despite the darkness, split her face from ear to ear like a gash to a watermelon. The impressive goggles sitting on her trumpet nose made her resemble an amphibian, the random result of a furtive coupling between an innocent young girl and a facetious toad. Other than the dress, the young girl accompanying her bore no family resemblance to her, except her strangeness. Even face on she seemed to be in profile, so thin and evanescent was her figure, shaped like a lengthy drip of candle wax.

'After all the rain we've had, it's good to have a breath of evening air.'

'That's true, it does you good.'

The stump of a woman looked up at the sky and immediately her immense glasses trapped the moon. It had risen, almost full, and cast a disturbing light through a reddish halo. Some anaemic stars were pecking around it.

'Might not last. We should enjoy it while we can, shouldn't we?'

'Tomorrow is another day.'

'You mustn't believe that, Monsieur. It's just the same one beginning over and over again.'

Monsieur Lavenant hadn't expected his banal comment to arouse such strong feeling in the short lady. She had grabbed hold of the garden gate with both hands so vehemently that it looked as if she was going to uproot it and go off with it. Confronted by the rubbery mask looming towards him, glasses daubed in moonlight, he shrank into his chair.

'You only live for a single day, Monsieur, just one! But it's the most beautiful one. I wish you good evening, Monsieur. Farewell.'

He saw them disappearing hand in hand at the corner of the road, leaving only a sort of echo of their presence. For a few seconds he wondered whether he might not have dreamed them, then went back indoors. Thérèse was just serving the lemon verbena tea.

'Thérèse, have you already come across the two women I've been talking to?'

'Which two women?'

'Two out for a walk. One tall, and one small with huge glasses. They had identical dresses, beige with blue flowers …'

'I wasn't watching, I was doing the washing up. Why?'

'No reason. You must have heard me talking to someone though?'

'I confess I didn't, with the tap running and the noise of the dishes. Is it important?'

'No, we just exchanged a few words about the weather, that's all.'

'It's quite usual to have a little after-dinner walk when the weather's so fine. We ought to take advantage of it more often. Be careful, the tea's boiling-hot.'

Monsieur Lavenant was having difficulty concentrating on his book. He read the same sentence for the tenth time and it still made no more sense to him than if it had been in Chinese. He saw, running through the pages like a watermark, sometimes the frog woman's face, sometimes that of the ectoplasm accompanying her. Uncertainty that they existed was bothering him like a wobbly tooth you wiggle with the tip of your tongue. He laid his book down open on his thigh and lit a cigarette, thinking to himself that it would take a lot more than a cup of lemon verbena tea to send him to sleep. Opposite him, wearing the cone of orangey light from the standard lamp as a hat, Thérèse sat, lips slightly parted, leafing through 1960s issues of *Paris Match*, which she must have dug out of the attic. There were trunks full of them, and also of *Ciné Revue*, *Elle* and other magazines Cécile had a liking for. An onlooker might have taken them for an old married couple. Had his wife not been dead, they would certainly have spent the evening in the same way. Cécile was beautiful, Thérèse was not, that was the only difference; that and the fact that today Cécile would be ten years older.

'Is it good?'

'I'm sorry?'

'The magazine, is it good?'

'Pfff … It's funny, it reminds me of my childhood: Martine Carol, Gina Lollobrigida, the Algerian war, the Peugeot 403, Saint-Tropez … It passes the time.'

'Are you bored here?'

'No more than elsewhere. It comes with the job.'

'Your work bores you?'

'That's not what I said. A little bit, sometimes, like everyone. That's normal.'

'I was never bored when I was working.'

'But you had worries.'

'True. But worries aren't the same as boredom. With worries, you always find a way of working things out, whereas with boredom it's another thing altogether.'

'You mean it's harder to work things out with yourself?'

'Yes. Obviously, with other people it's quite simple; they're always in the wrong, so you can argue, but when you're all alone, face to face with yourself in the mirror ...'

'I understand. Personally, I'm never bored by boredom. Listen, without boredom, no prisoner would ever think of digging a tunnel several kilometres long with a teaspoon in order to escape. There'd have been no Christopher Columbus discovering America. On a much smaller scale, how would I ever have left Colmar if I hadn't been bored to death there?'

This whole jumble of words descended on Monsieur Lavenant like a summer downpour. He would never have suspected Thérèse could hold that many. Everyone, this evening, seemed to know better than him.

'Why don't you speak to me like that more often?'

'Because you don't ask me to. Because it's not very important, I suppose.'

'I was wrong.'

Maybe it was an effect of the light, but Thérèse was no longer quite Thérèse and Monsieur Lavenant was less and less Monsieur Lavenant. In the closeness of silence, each of them was shedding the faded trappings the years had gradually covered them in.

'You know, my name is Édouard.'

'I know.'

'Ah … Perhaps you might call me Édouard instead of Monsieur.'

'If you wish. That's not a problem.'

'Good. It's easier, isn't it? It seems a little … old-fashioned.'

Thérèse locked her lavender eyes on his until he had to look away. He was no longer accustomed to such trials of strength. Generally it was other people who lowered their eyes in front of him. He had forgotten just how delicious it is to lose one's head, to lay down one's heavy rusted armour at the other's feet. Wiping his hand over his face to get a grip on himself, between his fingers he caught a glimpse of Thérèse's shoulder, her mouth and a lock of hair that lay across her brow. The desire rising in him could not be blamed on the lemon verbena tea.

'Maybe we should go to bed.'

'Together?'

Édouard felt a shiver run through him from head to toe, a seismic shock he didn't even try to contain.

'I'm an old man, you know.'

'You are a man and you need tenderness; I'm a woman, past my youth, and I need some too. I'm sorry, I don't know what came over me …'

Édouard held her close while, sniffing, she took hold of the tray.

'I'd be honoured, Thérèse, very honoured. Leave all that.'

They exchanged an awkward kiss, trembling so much that their teeth knocked together, and that made them laugh.

With his fingertips Monsieur Lavenant felt around for Thérèse's body. Nothing was left of her but her imprint on the crumpled sheet and one hair forming an initial on the pillow. It had to be very early nonetheless, as dawn was only just breaking. Invisible birds were chattering in the trees. He pulled the cover back up over his shoulders because there was still a touch of the night's chill in the air. He listened out but could hear no sound from either the bathroom or the kitchen. He was a little disappointed. He would have liked to surprise her sleeping. They hadn't made love but the tenderness they'd felt falling asleep in each other's arms was worth any number of orgasms. He was amazed that he didn't feel guilty, like he had every time he'd slept with women other than his wife. It was because this was in no way comparable. It wasn't about satisfying a sexual need, which in any case generally provided him with only mediocre satisfaction. He wasn't sleepy any more. An excitement like that of a child on Christmas morning bounced him out of bed. He wanted coffee, bread and jam, and to throw himself headlong into any activity whatsoever. He wanted to live.

Passing Thérèse's room, he heard the bed squeak. This morning he would be the one to prepare the breakfast.

Obviously, with only one arm, the whole business took some time and the results were somewhat haphazard. Thérèse appeared just as he swore at a stubborn jam-jar lid.

'What on earth are you doing?'

'The damn lid's stuck.'

'Never mind. Give it here or you'll do something silly.'

Usually when he came downstairs in the morning, he would find Thérèse washed and dressed, and well into her day's activities. Today she still bore the stigmata of sleep: ruffled hair, sticky eyelashes and pillow stripes scarifying her right cheek.

Grumpily, she took the jar out of his hands and urged him to go and sit down. She was the one who poured the coffee and spread the bread, without a word or a look.

'Good morning anyway!'

'Huh?'

'I said, good morning anyway.'

'Good morning.'

'What's the matter?'

'Nothing. It's just I don't think it's sensible for you to get involved with cooking. You could have been scalded or cut yourself. And anyway it's my job.'

'Why didn't you stay in my room?'

'Because I'm not used to sleeping with someone else.'

'Do I snore?'

'It's not that – though, yes, you do snore. Listen, let's be honest with each other. I'm not after your money. I'm very fond of you but you mustn't think … We got carried away yesterday evening. I don't regret it but we mustn't make a habit of it or …'

'Or what?'

'It wouldn't be the same.'

'So?'

'So? I wouldn't be me any longer, and you wouldn't be you. Besides, nothing happened, so let's leave it there. It's better that way. Why are you smiling?'

'You've got a coffee moustache at the corners of your mouth.'

'Very clever.'

Thérèse wiped her lips with her napkin. Her eyes were brimming with tears as she got to her feet. Édouard caught hold of her wrist before she could escape.

'Listen to me, Thérèse. I'm not trying to make you play the part of the priest's housekeeper. I feel comfortable with you and I believe you feel the same way. It's as simple as that. Whether we have a sexual relationship or not isn't important, you know, at my age … What matters is that for the first time in long years, I don't feel alone any more; that's to say I'm no longer the centre of a shrunken world, and humbly I feel able to give you that same gift, because although I know almost nothing about you, one thing I'm sure of is that you are much more familiar with this solitude than I am. There's no obligation on your part or mine; you can go on sleeping in your own room; we can continue to call each other "vous", but from now on, whatever you may do, there is a Thérèse and Édouard.'

With a squeeze of her fingers he let go of her hand, sensing that Thérèse was about to dissolve into tears and that she wanted to be alone to unburden herself of the pressure filling her chest.

Towards nine o'clock the sky had grown dark, leaden with thick banks of cloud like a herd of elephants. The electricity in the air made it impossible to stay in one place for five minutes. Monsieur Lavenant and Thérèse had done nothing but meet each other coming and going like two demented clockwork toys. The atmosphere was stifling; the air piled up in the lungs like a wad of grey cotton wool. Then on the dot of eleven a violent storm broke, the rain streaming down hastily shut windows. Noses pressed to the window panes, Thérèse and Édouard jumped in unison at each lightning flash that preceded the din of thunder. Édouard counted the seconds, one, two, three, four ... between the brilliant flashes and dull thuds which made the house shake.

'That one wasn't far away, four kilometres at the most. Above May, perhaps. It can't be much fun over there.'

The herd of elephants disappeared as it had come, leaving behind only a hammering noise on the eardrums, and a swollen sky above Rémuzat. A spider's web fringed with raindrops at the corner of the gutter glimmered like a diamond necklace.

'That might be enough, don't you think?'

'Yes ... No, wait, that one too, it's a giant.'

After the morning's storm, Édouard had taken it into his head to go and look for snails by the roadside. They'd collected far too many, more than they'd ever be able to eat, according to Thérèse, who with a sinking heart was contemplating the laborious preparation of the gastropods that lay ahead. But Édouard kept discovering ever bigger ones, with the result that the dozens were multiplying.

'Édouard, it's a waste. We're never going to be able to eat all those.'

'You're right. But it's such a long time since I went snailing … I must have been a young boy, I suppose.'

They set off peacefully for home, Édouard tickling the grasses on the verge with his walking stick, Thérèse carrying the slimy basket. The hot, humid earth was exhaling heady perfumes.

'When we get there, we'll purge the creatures and then go into town.'

'To Nyons? What for?'

'I need to buy a typewriter.'

'Ah.'

'And a ream of paper. There's no better age to write your memoirs than when you're losing your memory. Come on, let's go faster.'

On arriving back from Nyons, their arms full of a brand-new typewriter, two reams of paper (Monsieur Lavenant had so many memories) and some carbon paper, they had the pleasure of discovering the kitchen overrun by freedom-loving snails. The lid of the pail in which they'd been imprisoned along with two generous handfuls of coarse salt had not withstood the pressure from the escapees. They were everywhere. Some were bravely setting off up the north face of the fridge, while others, sensing where their career was to end, were clinging to the glass door of the oven, but most were just wandering around completely lost on the tiles, in total disarray. Streams of sticky slime were coming over the top of the pail and drying in silvery patches here and there. It took longer to catch and return them to their container than it had to collect them in the grass. While a grumbling Thérèse took a cloth to the floor, Édouard carefully unwrapped his work instrument, put on his glasses and began to give the instructions his most serious attention. At almost midnight, the table on which the machine took pride of place was surrounded by a sort of snowdrift of balls of crumpled paper with YYWW OOOOOOO ffff §§§§ … … +++++ … … nnnnn … … %%%%% or ///// printed on them. More than once Monsieur Lavenant had come very close to slinging the thing out of the window, having first crushed it with an iron. But thanks to Thérèse's cool head, they had finally managed to get it to tabulate correctly and produce more or less legible type.

'There now, we've done it.'

'Yes, but you must admit it's ridiculously complicated. I had a manual Olivetti for years and it never let me down.'

'It's the modern world. Just look at all the things you can do with this one: delete, save, make corrections …'

'But I'm not asking all that of the modern world. I'm quite capable of doing corrections myself, I'm not an invalid … OK, it's a figure of speech … Goodness, with all this we haven't had any dinner.'

After the frugal meal, Édouard went upstairs to clean his

teeth and put on his pyjamas, before stretching out on his bed in the dark, eyes wide open in spite of his fatigue. He hadn't dared ask Thérèse to join him, hoping she would do so of her own accord. Listening out, he could hear water running in the bathroom, and the washing process seemed interminable. Although he tried to stop himself falling asleep, his eyelids drooped inexorably and he yawned like a wild beast. He barely felt her slip between the sheets beside him and plant a very gentle kiss on his cheek.

'My name is Édouard Lavenant. I'll be seventy-five next October. I spent the night with my nurse. It was very ...' There followed a list of adjectives such as pleasant, nice, reassuring, tender, touching, all crossed out. The rest of the page was covered in scribbles, the kind doodled in biro during a telephone conversation. From his long years of existence, that was all he remembered and it dated from the evening before. There was no need to be put out by this, beginnings are always difficult. Monsieur Lavenant stretched in his chair and consulted his watch. Two hours of work, that wasn't too bad. He had taken the infernal machine up to his room where it was quieter. It looked good on the small desk, with the white pages adorning the carriage. A bunch of impeccably sharpened pencils stood alongside the dictionary, which was next to an ashtray already overflowing with cigarette ends. A real writer's table. He yawned so wide he could have dislocated his jaw.

Too late to bed. Out of practice. Too nervy. Strange dreams

where he was travelling in a narrow lift that never arrived at either the top or the bottom floor. Not nightmarish, merely boring. It was only in the early hours that he had been able to enjoy completely undisturbed sleep, and when he opened his eyes, Thérèse was no longer there. But that didn't matter, as he was sure she had spent the night with him. A whole night. The proof being that she had left her dressing gown and slippers at the end of the bed. He who had decided to immerse himself in the past was now interested in nothing but the present. Right, that was enough for the first day's work. He needed to stretch his legs, and thanks to sitting on that chair he had backache and wanted to pee. In short, he had every incentive to be elsewhere.

'Making progress?'

'Gently does it. You don't just dive into that sort of enterprise, you have to think; it takes time.'

'A bit like the snails then. That's five times I've rinsed them and there's still loads of slime! That was a great idea you had there.'

'I'll see to the court-bouillon.'

'No, leave it, it's fine. I'll manage better on my own.'

Behind the grumpy front, Thérèse was smiling, while her reddened hands were moving the shells in the stream of water. Édouard went over and awkwardly stroked her hair. She turned in amazement and he put his hand down again, blushing.

'I'm going to buy cigarettes. Do you need anything?'

'Butter, please. I'm worried about having enough.'

Aside from the buzzing of the flies and the inevitable sputtering of a machine somewhere in the distance, there was no noise in the village. In spite of the tinted lenses in his spectacles, the contrast between areas of light and shadow was painful on the eyes. Monsieur Lavenant felt as if he were moving in an old silent home movie with a jumping black-and-white picture, random changes of speed and occasional white flashes where the film had melted, eaten away by a luminous leprosy.

As he went through the narrow streets, the ground-floor shutters seemed to half open to allow a split-second glimpse of a Goyaesque figure looming out of the darkness. A cat jumped down from a wall and crossed the road, glaring at him with blazing eyes, before taking up another strategic position. He was forced to step over a horribly fat dog, as dirty as a pig, which was slumped in the middle of the pavement, snoring. Apart from these two mammals he didn't meet a living soul until he reached the tobacconist's. The cool breath of a fan caressed his face as soon as he had passed the curtain of multicoloured strips which kept flies out of the shop. During the two or three minutes before the tobacconist's leisurely appearance, Monsieur Lavenant, like a child in Ali Baba's cave, was seized by an overwhelming desire to treat himself to something, anything – a postcard, a ball, a badminton set, a fishing rod.

Back on the pavement, with his cigarettes in his pocket and his fishing rod under his arm, he felt a strange mixture of pride and shame. If he'd wanted to go in for the sport seriously, he could have bought himself a decidedly more sophisticated piece of equipment. He'd tried his hand at it, salmon in Scotland, big fish in the Pacific, but no, it was this rod, this child's bamboo cane with its cheap little reel, its line, and its two-coloured float in a neat plastic packet which had taken his fancy. It was more than likely that he'd never use it, but so what? It had brought him pleasure and, drunk on his own daring, he sat down on the café terrace in the completely deserted square and ordered a barley water.

'Are you going fishing?'

'No, it's a present for my grandson. How much do I owe you?'

'The same as usual; my prices haven't changed.'

What was that supposed to mean, 'the same as usual'? It was the first time he'd set foot in the place. There was some mistake, the chap had confused him with a regular. Plus, why were the waiter and the tobacconist as alike as two peas in a pod? The same stocky build, same steel wool on the cheeks, same shifty look ... Brothers, no doubt. In such a small village it's not unusual to see members of the same family running different businesses ... Monsieur Lavenant chased away his question marks with a large gulp of barley water. The ice cube banging against his teeth was like hitting an iceberg. He must have been seven or eight when he'd first gone fishing, with his uncle, Bernard ... No, not Bernard, Roland, yes, Roland! Or maybe Martial? A fat man, at any rate, who laughed all the time and whom his mother thought vulgar. Édouard had kept his eyes on his float the whole day without catching a single fish. When he went for a pee, he'd looked over his shoulder and seen his uncle hooking a roach to the end of his fishing line. 'Édouard, come quickly! You've got a bite.'

Not only had that not brought him pleasure, he'd felt humiliated by it. That evening he hadn't touched the fried fish.

Monsieur Lavenant mopped his brow with his handkerchief. He could still see the scene clearly and yet he could have sworn that this memory didn't belong to him. He was no longer as certain as all that of having been fishing with an uncle, Bernard, Roland or Martial, nor of having gone fishing in Scotland or the Pacific, nor whether he'd drunk barley water on this terrace before … Apart from the fishing rod, whose bamboo pole he was clutching in his fist so tightly it might break, he was no longer sure of anything.

In front of him, without his noticing, a group of boules players had magically sprung up in the square. The boules knocked into one another and laughter erupted: 'Oh Daniel, you're not even trying.' On the benches in the shade old women were quietly knitting new rows in long-running quarrels. A little boy was going round and round in circles on his tricycle. They all bore a striking family resemblance to the tobacconist and waiter. Monsieur Lavenant wondered whether his left arm hadn't perhaps contaminated the rest of him, he had so much difficulty getting up from his chair. As stiffly as Pinocchio he crossed the square and vanished into the maze of narrow streets. The butter, he had to get some butter … But where was the minimarket? Where was he himself, come to that? And why did he have to get butter?

And why did his mother find his uncle vulgar? And why was this fishing rod under his arm? He had to lean against a wall, tears in his eyes, lungs choked by a cry which couldn't escape, a cry which came from far, far away, from the very pit of his stomach …

'Good day, Monsieur. Enjoying your walk?' The woman with the rubber mask turned her unfathomable gaze on him. Two steps behind her stood the gangling young woman, pale as a shadow on a negative.

'It's stupid, I can't find my way …'

'It's not a very big place!'

'I know, but a few months ago I had a stroke … an illness … I don't know …'

'Don't worry, we'll walk you home. Give me your arm.'

The touch of the woman's skin on his own chilled him. It felt like marble. The tall girl walked along behind them like a faithful spaniel, without blinking once.

'I'm sorry, this is the first time …'

'It happens to us all … Don't worry, we're only five minutes from your house. Are you a fisherman?'

'No, no, it's for … a child.'

'He'll like it, I'm sure. All children love fishing, even if they generally hate fish. Children are a bit cruel. I knew a charming one, who ripped off …'

Monsieur Lavenant didn't understand a word of what the woman was saying. His body was now nothing more than a sack stuffed with cotton wool, incapable of the slightest initiative. Not until he saw the familiar steps concertinaing up to his doorstep did Monsieur Lavenant recover his wits.

'I'm most grateful to you for accompanying me. May I offer you a cold drink?'

'That's very kind of you but we have to get back. Another time. Good evening, Monsieur.'

'Good evening, Mesdames.'

He watched them as far as the street corner, where they dematerialised in the rays of the setting sun.

'What on earth have you been up to then? It's almost three hours since you left. And what about the butter?'

'I'm sorry, I couldn't find the minimarket. Really sorry.'

'It doesn't matter, but I was worried … What's that?'

'A fishing rod.'

'Are you taking up fishing?'

'I don't think so. It's a child's one.'

Thérèse watched as he laid the rod on the table and slumped into a chair. The expression 'shadow of his former self' suggested itself to her immediately.

He seemed to be sitting just to one side of his body, like a transfer applied by a shaky hand.

'I haven't put them back in their shells.'

'I'm sorry?'

'The snails, I didn't put them back in their shells – I've done little ramekins. It's less work, and easier for you to eat.'

'Good idea, Thérèse.'

'And it tastes just as good.'

Monsieur Lavenant hadn't so much as poked his nose outside the door for three days, and was communicating only in monosyllables – yes, no – completely haphazardly. Occasionally his words hit the mark, but more often than not they didn't, which had a way of really exasperating Thérèse. 'Look, I'd prefer it if you didn't say anything at all!' He was scarcely more voluble at his keyboard. While waiting for 'it' to come, he would try on words like hats, in upper and lower case, dipping into the dictionary at random in the vain hope of finding one which would be the key to his sealed-off memory. None existed, however, for the simple reason that his past didn't interest him in the least. Everything in it was drab, faded, without colour or scent. He had come to the conclusion that any life at all was worth more than his. Even the best moments were coated with that obstinate dust which inspires you not to take up a pen but to resort to clearing the attic. He wanted none other than to be reborn, virgin, nothing behind him, nothing ahead, to learn everything afresh. He had noticed that if you typed the same word all over a whole page, that word ended up losing its meaning completely. Only an empty wrapper was left, which could be filled with some completely different sense. PIANO, PIANO, PIANO, PI-A-NO, PI-A-NO! The repeated experiment plunged him into a state of strange exaltation. Today he had just wrung the life out of the word PUGNACIOUS and derived the serene satisfaction of having done his duty. It was exhausting work, and a real marathon, when you considered that the Petit Larousse contained 58,900 common nouns. But the game was worth the candle; when he had unlearned everything he would be entitled to a completely new life.

Switching off the typewriter, he laid the PUGNACIOUS page on top of the PIANO one. He stood up, rubbing his back. Thérèse's nightdress cascaded over the back of the chair. He noted CASCADE on a pad, in pencil. That was tomorrow's word.

'Édouard? ... Monsieur Lavenant?'

'Yes?'

'Someone's here asking for you.'

Thérèse was waiting for him at the foot of the stairs, frowning.

'It's a gentleman.'

'What does he want?'

'He says it's personal.'

'Oh.'

'He's waiting in the sitting room.'

As in a doctor's waiting room, when Édouard came in, the man put the magazine he was flicking through down on the coffee table, got to his feet and held out his hand. He must have been around forty, tall, slim and well turned out.

'Jean-Baptiste Lorieux.'

'To what do I owe the pleasure?'

'The name Lorieux doesn't ring any bells?'

'Lorieux? No, I don't think so.'

'That doesn't surprise me. I'm Sylvie Lorieux's son …'

'That doesn't mean anything to me either.'

'I understand. We're going back about forty years. Sylvie Lorieux was your secretary at that time.'

Monsieur Lavenant narrowed his gaze. The man's face was strangely familiar but he couldn't see the slightest trace of a Sylvie Lorieux coming through.

'Don't rack your brains, I'll explain. I'm a communications consultant and by the greatest coincidence I found myself working for your firm in Lyon. My mother often spoke about you. For a long time I was in two minds about meeting you, then … well, here I am.'

'I don't quite grasp the purpose of your visit.'

'I'm your son.'

When it was hot, Sylvie Lorieux used to put her hair up in a chignon, held in place by a pencil. She was a pretty girl, gentle, discreet. They had spent only one night together, during a business trip to Brussels. A simple one-night stand. Some months later she had left her job. He no longer remembered the reason. He'd missed her as she was very competent. Sylvie Lorieux.

'Sit down. How is your mother?'

'She died. Four years ago.'

'Oh, I'm sorry. Have you known for long that …'

'Yes. Since I was old enough to understand.'

'And you never tried to contact me?'

'Yes, once. I must have been sixteen or seventeen. I phoned. It was your wife who answered. I hung up.'

'Were you living in Lyon?'

'No, Paris.'

The silence uniting the two men was short-lived. The merciless neighbour had just started up one of his diabolical machines. As Monsieur Lavenant got up to shut the window, Thérèse knocked on the door.

'I have to go out for some shopping – you don't need anything, do you?'

'No, thank you, Thérèse.'

She stayed for a moment, surreptitiously giving him a questioning look, and then, receiving no sign from him, closed the door behind her, but not before she'd given the stranger a dark stare. Monsieur Lavenant sat down in his armchair again, lighting a cigarette to give himself time to think of something to say.

'I find it a little hard to believe you. The relationship I had with your mother – can it really be called a relationship? – was extremely short.'

'I know, she told me. Once is enough though. That being so, she never blamed you for anything. I think she was really very much in love with you. There was your wife, however. She chose to leave the scene.'

'She never married?'

'No. The odd boyfriend. I never felt she missed the past.

She had good memories of you. I believe she had quite a happy life.'

'You … Were you ever in need?'

'I wanted for nothing.'

'Not even a father?'

'To be honest, no. Well, sometimes, maybe. Most of my friends were fighting with theirs. It doesn't make you wish for one.'

'So why did you want to meet me after all this time?'

'In Lyon I discovered that you'd been seriously ill. I think I would have regretted not having known you.'

Monsieur Lavenant gave a bitter little laugh.

'Sorry, but I've already made my will, and anyway, as you can see, apart from this crippled arm I'm in the best of health.'

'I *knew* you'd think of that. You're mistaken. I make a very good living, I don't need money.'

'Come on! You'd be the only one then. I'm warning you, I'll categorically refuse to take any test of my supposed paternity.'

'You've got it wrong. As I've already said, it's not a question of that. I needed to see you, the way one needs to look at oneself in a mirror, to follow a river upstream to its source.'

'Very poetic, I'm sure, but you've happened on a stagnant pool. What do you expect me to do with a son at my age? Bounce you up and down on my knee?'

'I'm sorry. You're right, I'm on the wrong track. I'm sorry for disturbing you.'

Jean-Baptiste stood up, hesitated, then held out his hand to Édouard. It was a hand as honest and wholesome as a slice of bread.

'Oh sit down, for heaven's sake! I'm not sending you away. You parachute in like this, without a word of warning ... Are you going back up to Lyon?'

'No, I'm on my way to Avignon. That's why I made the detour. I have a meeting tomorrow, in the early afternoon.'

'So you're free for the day?'

'Yes.'

'Then you'll stay to lunch. I won't take no for an answer.'

When Thérèse came back from shopping, Édouard introduced Jean-Baptiste as an employee of his firm, and she seemed relieved. During the meal they talked work, percentages, profits and losses, things Thérèse didn't understand but which in a way reassured her. When this Monsieur Lorieux had turned up that morning, she had been struck at once by his family resemblance to Édouard and, without really knowing why, had thought it augured badly. Now she was cross with herself for her misgivings. The man was most polite, calm, something of a dreamer. Édouard seemed pleased to have met him. In contrast to the previous days, he was talkative, full of a verve which took years off him. Even so, that resemblance ... She left them to have coffee in the garden and went off to attend to other tasks.

The shadow of the lime tree cast a myriad of ever-changing patterns on the white tablecloth. A bee prowled round the sugar bowl. Édouard and Jean-Baptiste had started talking about business only to put Thérèse off the scent. At present they didn't really know what to say to each other, both of them afraid of lapsing into the worst banalities.

'Do you like fishing?'

'Sorry?'

'Angling, do you like it?'

'I don't know. I've never tried. I've always lived in a city.'

'Not even on holiday though?'

'No. It never appealed. Do you fish?'

'Once upon a time. Do you feel like it?'

'Now?'

'Yes, why not? There are fish in the Aygues. I bought a rod yesterday. Why not sleep here tonight? With an early start you'll have plenty of time to get to Avignon for the early afternoon.'

'Why not? I have to admit I wasn't expecting that, but …'

'Did I expect to have a son?'

The stone was red-hot in the place Édouard had chosen, a two- to three-metre overhang above a pool just after a little waterfall. He had discovered the spot during a walk; you could see fish the size of your hand swimming back and forth in the clear water. After explaining to Jean-Baptiste how to prepare his line, he had sat slightly further back, where the branches of a willow formed a shelter. His son had square shoulders; his white shirt was so dazzling in the sun that Édouard had to pull the brim of his hat down over his eyes.

'If someone had told me this morning that I'd be going fishing with my father …'

'If we knew everything about the future, the present wouldn't be worth a jot. Are you married?'

'Yes.'

'Children?'

'Two. Richard's nine and Noémie turns six next month.'

'So I'm a grandfather?'

'You certainly are.'

'Have you told them about me?'

'No, and my wife doesn't know either.'

'Will you tell them?'

'I don't know. What do you think?'

'Don't turn round. Keep your eyes on your float … You should do what you want. It makes no difference to me. I'm not family-minded. What's your wife's name?'

'Nelly.'

'So all in all, you're a happy man?'

'You could say that. What are those birds up above the mountain? Buzzards?'

'No, vultures.'

'Vultures, here?'

'Yes, griffon vultures.'

'I'm out fishing with my son. I have a daughter-in-law called Nelly and two grandchildren. It's grotesque! Children steal your past in order to make their own present from it; they take you apart like an old alarm clock and leave you in bits.

Vultures at least have the decency to wait until their prey is dead before they rip it to pieces. Secondary tumours, that's what they are, reproducing themselves ad infinitum. I didn't want to leave anything behind me, not a thing! What do you have to do to finally be at peace? To stop dragging the past around like a ball and chain? I was just beginning to feel lighter, then this idiot fetches up with his healthy looks, his good intentions and his nice little family. He can go to hell!'

His hand tightened around a large stone, as smooth and round as an egg.

'That's it! I've got one! What do I do now?'

Monsieur Lavenant let go of the pebble. Jean-Baptiste was wrestling with his line, at the end of which wriggled a gleaming fish.

'Well, you unhook it and throw it back into the water. They're inedible, these fish, packed full of bones.'

Jean-Baptiste had gone to fetch his bag from the car, carrying the fishing rod – a gift from Monsieur Lavenant – under his arm. Thérèse was in the garden reading, feet up on a chair. Seeing Édouard coming, she lowered her dress, which she had hitched halfway up her thighs.

'Has Monsieur Lorieux left?'

'He's gone to fetch his things. He'll have dinner with us and spend the night here.'

'Oh?'

'Yes. What's so surprising in that? There's no hotel here. He's leaving for Avignon early tomorrow morning.'

'Oh, it doesn't bother me, it's just that I have to get a room ready for him and change my menu. I think he's a very likeable young man, very well brought up. It's unbelievable how much he resembles you; he's like you as a young man.'

'What do you know about it? You never knew me when I was young.'

'I'm imagining ...'

'Well, you imagine wrong. I wasn't at all like that. I'm going to take a shower.'

With a towel round his waist, Édouard faced himself in the bathroom mirror. 'No, I wasn't at all like that. No one thought I was likeable. I was already a dried-up old stick. I didn't look like my father, short and stout with such dull eyes. I've always suspected my mother must have been unfaithful to him, even if she would never admit it to me. It's better to be no one's son than just anybody's.'

Slowly the steam turned the mirror opaque and Monsieur Lavenant was relieved to be back in the limbo he should never have left.

Thérèse had been behaving flirtatiously all evening. She and Jean-Baptiste seemed to get along extremely well. He had done his military service near Strasbourg and knew Alsace like the back of his hand. Monsieur Lavenant thought her ridiculous in the lilac dress he had never seen her wearing before. He felt sidelined, relegated to the rank of aged relation whom people respect, admittedly, while keeping a surreptitious eye on his wine and cigarette consumption. Thérèse and Jean-Baptiste had just discovered something else they had in common, besides Alsace. They had the same birthday. Wasn't that amazing? They'd just missed spending their birthday together! Monsieur Lavenant insisted on cracking open a bottle of champagne, even though the other two didn't see the need.

'Yes, yes! It's not every day you have something to celebrate. I'll go down to the cellar.'

Édouard sat on a packing case, staring at the naked forty-watt light bulb hanging from the vaulted ceiling. There was a smell of humus, mushrooms, the dark. So that was where he'd be spending eternity, while the others danced on his head, eating, drinking, making love, laughing in honour of that bitch, life. How could all that continue without him? There was still too much light in this crypt. Wielding the bottle like a club, he smashed the bulb. Groping his way, he dragged himself up the slippery steps and out of the cellar, like one of the living dead in a horror film.

Thérèse had cleared the table. Her cheeks were flushed, her eyes shining. With his back to them, Jean-Baptiste was holding both window panes wide open, breathing in the blue pigment of the night. On the ground his shadow made the shape of a large cross.

'Well now, where were you? You've been ages.'

'The cellar light's not working.'

They drank to the health of who knows what, health itself perhaps, before Thérèse disappeared, leaving father and son face to face.

'Thérèse is a very warm person. She seems very fond of

you.'

'She's competent.'

'No more than that?'

'That's all I want from her.'

Jean-Baptiste bent his head, then brought it up again immediately, with a serious look on his face.

'Are you angry with me for coming?'

'Tomorrow you'll have gone.'

'I don't understand you. One minute you're open, the next closed up, and I never know which side of the door I'm on.'

'Who's asking you to understand me? Am I trying to understand you? Anyway, what is there to understand? You wanted to see me, you've seen me, job done.'

Jean-Baptiste drained his glass and put it on the coffee table, damp-eyed.

'You're harsh, and it's taking a lot of effort to be like that. I'm sorry for you.'

'Oh please. I haven't asked for anything from you. And why should I deserve pity more than you? My life has been what it's been; it's as good as any other. I shall leave it with remorse, perhaps, but without regrets. Yours is just beginning, a little grub of a life that you're feeding with your illusions of a man in his prime. What a load of shit! No matter what you achieve – success in society, a happy family – it will all blow up in your face just as it does for the most heinous criminal. No, Monsieur Lorieux, I am not to be pitied, any more than any other human being.'

'How black your view of the world is.'

'If you think white is preferable then go and live on the ice fields. Everything's white over there – the igloos, the bears, the polar nights! There's no one there any more; even the Eskimos have cleared off.'

'I wouldn't like to be like you at the end of my life.'

'There's no danger of that happening to you. Right, I think we've said all we had to say. I'm tired, I'm going to bed. Has Thérèse shown you your room?'

'Yes. We won't see each other again, then?'

'I don't see the need.'

'I'd have liked to do something for you.'

'The harm's been done, thanks. Goodnight.'

Monsieur Lavenant had had a bad night. Around four in the morning a cat fight had broken out on the roof of the shed next to his bedroom window. Starting off with threatening growls, it had turned into a stampede that set the old Roman tiles rattling, and culminated in an explosion of shrill miaowing which had reduced what remained of the night to tatters. He hadn't been able to shut his eyes again until almost six, and then only to marinate in a feverish half-sleep which had exhausted him more than if he'd stayed awake. It took him some time to clear his head of the shredded remnants of his dreams.

Entering the kitchen, he was astonished to see Jean-Baptiste busy washing his hands in the sink, motor oil up to his elbows.

'You're still here?'

'My car's broken down. I've just spent an hour trying to get it started, but no joy.'

'Oh.'

Édouard turned his back and poured himself a bowl of coffee. He didn't want his son to see the secret satisfaction on his face. Not because of his engine problems but because he was still there. He couldn't have said why.

'May I use your phone to call a mechanic?'

'Yes, but round here the mechanics are more often off fishing or hunting than in their garage. Worth a try though!'

He gestured towards the phone with his chin and began sipping his coffee, eyes level with the curved rim of the bowl. Without appearing to, he pricked up his ears.

'What, three at the earliest? Well, give me the address of one of your colleagues. Oh … well, in that case … Yes, I'll manage somehow, thanks.'

While Jean-Baptiste suffered defeat after defeat with the car mechanics, a broad smile was spreading across Édouard's face. Naturally his mouth reverted to its usual downward curve when his son came and sat down opposite him, chewing his thumbnail.

'You couldn't make it up! They all have urgent breakdowns.'

'What did I tell you? A little coffee?'

'Yes please.'

'I think you might not make your meeting in Avignon.'

'My meeting? Oh, yes. To tell you the truth, I haven't got a meeting in Avignon.'

'What?'

'No. My wife's taken the children to her parents' for a few days. I took advantage of the break to come and see you.'

'So you're not in a hurry?'

'Not especially.'

'Do you often tell lies, Monsieur Lorieux?'

'Of course not! I needed a pretext, that's all.'

74

'Butter me a piece of bread, would you? I can't manage it with one hand.'

Édouard was taking a mischievous delight in the situation. Jean-Baptiste was really just a big kid caught with his finger in the jam jar.

'Not too much honey! Just a spoonful or else it gets everywhere. Thank you. Isn't Thérèse here?'

'She's gone to the market. We had breakfast together.'

'What do you think you'll do?'

'What do you expect me to do? Wait three hours for the mechanic to get here. I'll go for a walk. Is there a good restaurant here?'

'No. There are two, both equally appalling.'

'Oh well, too bad. I'll make do.'

Monsieur Lavenant lit a cigarette and voluptuously blew smoke towards the ceiling.

'Do you know how to make rings?' he asked.

'Sorry?'

'Smoke rings. Can you blow them?'

'No. I've never tried.'

'You should start now; it takes a while. Make your mouth into an "O" and let a little smoke come through; keep it there for a moment until it's quite dense and then send it out in short bursts with your glottis, raising your chin like so.'

A series of blueish rings issued from Édouard's lips and hovered for a while before dispersing as they hit the ceiling beams.

'Amazing, isn't it?'

'Very impressive.'

'It works better with cigars; almost perfect rings. I used to be quite an attraction at the end of a meal. What about whistling with your fingers, can you do that?'

'I ... I don't think so.'

'Whatever did your mother teach you? Place your thumb and index finger in the corners of your mouth, there, like so. Bend your tongue back as if you were about to swallow it and then blow ... Harder! Again!'

Jean-Baptiste was turning bright red but all that came out of his mouth was a damp hissing sound. Meanwhile opposite him Édouard was producing a range of shrill sounds which would have made many a young rascal green with envy. It was like a wildlife documentary, the old blackbird teaching his fledgling son to warble. Just at that moment Thérèse opened the door.

'What on earth's going on here? I could hear you all the way down the street! You're still here, Monsieur Lorieux?'

For an instant both men froze, fingers in their mouths, before Monsieur Lavenant stood up, taut as a bow.

'Monsieur Lorieux's car's broken down. I was teaching him to whistle. He'll be having lunch with us. I'm going up for my shower.'

The mechanic let the bonnet drop and wiped his hands on an oily rag, shaking his head.

'Very strange ... In theory a bit like that never goes ...'

'Is it bad?'

'No, but I haven't got the part. I'll need to get it sent from Lyon.'

'Will it take long?'

'Well … Five o'clock now. If I order it straight away, I'll have it for tomorrow afternoon. By the time it's fitted … tomorrow evening, maybe?'

Unable to make up his mind, Jean-Baptiste rubbed his chin, eyeing his car as if it were a UFO. Behind him Monsieur Lavenant was growing impatient.

'You've got no choice. Leave your car to this gentleman here and let that be an end to it. You're in for another night at our house, that's all. Isn't that so, Thérèse?'

'Monsieur Lavenant's right, there's nothing else for it.'

'I'm so embarrassed …'

'Oh, come on, no fuss please. You'll have your car back tomorrow, no need to make a big thing of it. Let's go home. There's no point in standing here.'

Jean-Baptiste handed over his keys to the mechanic and all three of them started for home. If the son seemed upset, the father was visibly in an excellent mood. Between the two, Thérèse didn't know which attitude she should adopt.

'Come on, no need for that face. You've your whole life ahead of you – that's what you said, isn't it? Look, I'll buy you an aperitif.'

Thérèse was startled. 'But it's barely five o'clock.'

Thérèse had a strawberry and vanilla ice cream, Jean-Baptiste a beer and Monsieur Lavenant a *perroquet* because the lurid green cocktail suited his mood so well. In the square, the shadows of the plane trees made large mauve patches like continents on the dusty ground. According to a changeless ritual, the same scene was played out every day at the same time with the same actors: the boules players in their shorts, caps and old shoes, the old women gossiping on a bench amid the murmur of bees, and the little kid pedalling his tricycle like a maniac. Monsieur Lavenant gave a little laugh.

'Have you noticed?'

'What?'

'They all look alike, the old women, the boules players, the kid, the café owner. All from the same family.'

'Do you think so?'

'Of course, Thérèse. You can't miss it. Isn't that right, Lorieux?'

'It hadn't struck me, but now ...'

'It's obvious! They've all come from one stock, the mechanic as well; that nose, those ears ...'

'The mechanic had an Italian accent.'

'So? What does that prove? His father's second or third wife might have been Italian. Besides, you're annoying me, Thérèse, questioning everything all the time! If I say they're all from one family it's because I have good reason for it. If there's one thing I know about, it's family!'

'No need to get on your high horse. It's nothing to me whether they belong to the same family or not.'

'Obviously. You wouldn't know what that is; you've never had one.'

Thérèse's periwinkle gaze clouded and she turned away. Édouard drained his glass as if he wanted to swallow the nasty little words again. 'I'm sorry, Thérèse. I don't know what came over me. Besides, I've never been one for family. That gregarious need to be part of a whole has always been intolerable to me. We are born alone, we die alone and in between we act as if we're not. Oh, Lorieux, the vultures! Look how they soar ...'

A dozen raptors were initialling the sky with their wing tips above the Rocher du Caire. They didn't know how to laugh or cry, didn't wonder about birth or death, they just ate, slept, reproduced but above all they soared.

'Lorieux, how would you like to go and see them at closer quarters tomorrow morning? I've got excellent binoculars. It really is something to see, I assure you.'

'I'd love to.'

'Will you take us up there tomorrow morning, Thérèse?'

'Of course.'

'Perfect. Tell me, Lorieux, do you play boules?'

'It has been known, but I'm no expert.'

'I'll buy some straight away. I wonder why I didn't think of it earlier; it's one of the only sports I can play. The tobacconist nearby sells them. I'll be right back. We'll have a game tonight in the street, before dinner.'

Monsieur Lavenant leapt up and disappeared round the corner of the square, leaving Thérèse and Jean-Baptiste a little disconcerted.

'Is he often like this?'

'No, not really. For the last week he's been acting strangely. I think he's happy that you're here. He's behaving like a young man. With me, his life's a bit monotonous. Sometimes he's clumsy but it's because he's not used to it.'

'Used to what?'

'Being happy, I think.'

The boules were sold in pairs in a woven leather bag or in sixes in a wooden case with a jack and a square of chamois leather. They gleamed, nickel-plated and incised with different patterns, in their casket lined with midnight-blue velvet. They were like rare pearls. Édouard felt the weight of one before delicately putting it back.

'I'll take them. They're suitable, I mean, the weight …'

'I'll say so! Monsieur Drisse, our local champion, never uses anything else. He's won three trophies with them so that just shows you.'

Édouard left the tobacconist's to the tinkling of the little bell which marked customers' entrances and exits. Just at that moment a ray of sun striking the windscreen of a passing car dazzled him so much that he almost lost his balance. When he opened his eyes, everything was white, incandescent, motionless, as if turned to glass. The noises he could hear were no longer identifiable, compressed into one block of sound. He was suddenly overcome by a feeling of extreme loneliness, survivor's anguish. 'There's no one left. There's never been anyone … except me.' Death seemed a thousand times preferable to this prison existence. The boules weighed a ton. He took one step and then another, not to go anywhere as there was nowhere to go in this arid desert, but simply to start moving again.

'Is something wrong, Monsieur? Not well again?'

Édouard put his hand up to shade his eyes. Before him stood the two women, backs to the light, under the shadow of an enormous umbrella.

'Where are the others?'

'The others? People, you mean? Over there, of course, outside the café as usual.'

'Oh. For a moment I felt I was alone in the world, a sort of survivor. It was awful …'

'I know what you mean. That often happens to me; I'm an insomniac. Not being able to shut your eyes when everything around you is sleeping is a terrible trial. But don't worry, everyone's just where they should be. You've bought boules! They're lovely … For the child again?'

'Um, yes.'

'You're spoiling him. That's what children are for. Look at that one, pedalling his tricycle like a little racing driver. Isn't he sweet?'

For a few seconds they watched the little boy as he whirled around, head down, nose to the handlebars of his little trike, raising clouds of white dust.

'Pity they have to grow up. Well, we've got things to do. Have a good day, Monsieur.'

They vanished as they had appeared, in an overexposed patch of light.

Édouard had to make a great effort to hide his emotion

when he found Jean-Baptiste and Thérèse again on the café terrace.

'Is something wrong?'

'No, I'm fine.'

'If you want me to make a meal worthy of the name we really need to go now.'

No sooner had they stood up than there was a squeal of brakes from the main road, followed by an almost imperceptible thud which nevertheless froze everyone in a silent scream. The driver of the articulated lorry leapt down from his cab and rushed over to the body of the child, whose mangled tricycle lay there, one of its wheels still spinning. As if everything were being sucked out of the square, the boules players, the old women, the café owner and everyone rushed to the crash site. Only Édouard, Thérèse and Jean-Baptiste hung back. Someone said, 'It was bound to happen.'

Thérèse claimed to have a letter to write, in order to leave the two men alone in the garden. The night was balmy, lacquered. From her seat at the little desk she couldn't see them but through the window she could hear their voices clearly, rising with the drifts of cigarette smoke. She had realised that they were linked by more than just a professional relationship but she couldn't have said what. Besides, she didn't want to discover the secret. Far from feeling excluded by their complicity she felt quite touched at seeing them circling round each other with the awkwardness of two young puppies, Édouard twice as eccentric and Jean-Baptiste mired in his shyness. Sometimes when the two of them got lost in mutual incomprehension, she was the one they turned to, seeking a reliable mooring in her presence. Aware of her role as go-between, she would calm them with just a word or a smile. She felt useful, and that was enough for her.

Not having anyone to write to, she naturally began her letter with 'My dear Thérèse …' then, pen poised in mid-air, allowed herself to be lulled by the murmur from the garden.

'Have you any photos of your children?'

'No.'

'But that's the done thing. All fathers have photos of their children in their wallets.'

'Not me.'

'Nor of your wife?'

'Nor of her.'

'That's a shame. I'd have liked to see them. Do they look like you?'

'Who?'

'Your children!'

'Oh … I don't know. People say they do. For that you'd have to know what kind of face I have.'

'Mine, according to Thérèse.'

'It's hard with small children, they change all the time. Between taking the photo and getting it developed, they're already different.'

'And your wife, what's she like?'

'Oh well, blonde, average height, brown eyes …'

'You don't seem to be madly in love with her.'

'What makes you say that?'

'You're giving me an identikit description. What about your job? Do you like it?'

'I get good results, I think I'm quite competent.'

'A charmed life, all in all?'

'Do you turn into a pain in the arse at this time every night?'

'Ah, finally some bad language! A hint of rebellion and of sincerity. I'd given up hope of that. Shall I tell you something? You've no children, any more than you've a wife, and what's more, you don't work for my company. Don't deny it. I phoned my offices the day you got here. Not known at this address. You've lied to me all along except about one thing. I'm sure you're my son.'

Thérèse spat out the little bits of plastic from the ballpoint she had been chewing. The silence that followed this revelation made the darkness turn pale.

'What have you come here for?'

'I came out of prison a week ago. Maman died while I was inside. I didn't know where to go. I went by your offices and they told me where you were.'

'But why all these lies?'

'I wanted you to like me.'

'You've succeeded there! And what got you into prison?'

'Fraud. I worked for the Banque Nationale de Paris. I got five years.'

'I'm wondering whether I should believe you. In the end, I couldn't care less. Lie for lie, I prefer that one to the pathetic little life that was supposed to win me over. Have you any more nice surprises like that up your sleeve?'

'No, that's all.'

'Pity, it was just starting to get exciting! And what is it you expect from me? A word of apology? Power of attorney over my bank account?'

'Nothing. Nothing at all, I swear to you.'

'So things are fine as they are?'

'I'm really stuck. I haven't any friends or family. My whole life revolved around Maman. We were a sort of couple, like two shipwreck survivors on a desert island. She was always ill.

My work suffered … but I wanted to make her comfortable at the end of her life, beside the sea, far away from the lousy one-bedroom flat where we lived in Batignolles. I wanted to give her some fresh air before she died. Fresh air, do you see?'

'Please, spare me the violins. It might make them cry in the stalls, but not here. You're a failure. Full stop, end of. Tomorrow, in memory of your mother, if you haven't cut my throat between now and then, I'll write you a cheque and you can go and get yourself hanged elsewhere.'

'But I don't care about your sodding money! Don't you understand anything? What have you got inside that cage of bones, under all that wrinkled skin? Old bastard!'

'Little prick!'

Monsieur Lavenant didn't recognise Thérèse's voice when she shouted 'ÉDOUARD!' It seemed to come from deep inside himself, an echo that stopped him in his tracks as he was about to slap his son.

'Édouard, get up here immediately!'

He looked at his hand as if it belonged to someone else and let his arm fall, while Jean-Baptiste looked straight into his eyes, pale, lip trembling. A light came on in one of his neighbour's windows and the silhouette of a man with a bare chest appeared, like a shadow puppet.

'Stop that racket!'

Édouard gave a shrug and went up the steps to the door. Jean-Baptiste lit a cigarette and disappeared into the shrubbery.

Thérèse was standing on the doorstep, unbending as justice, and looking daggers at Édouard.

'How dare you shout at me like that in front of a stranger?'

'A stranger? I heard everything. You're hateful. From tomorrow you'll do without my services. I'm leaving you.'

'Why? What have I done to you?'

'To me? Nothing. But it's shameful to see a father humiliate his son like that.'

'My son, my son ... a liar, a crook, a thief! Two days ago I didn't even know he existed. You think someone becomes a father in forty-eight hours?'

'That's not the point, he's a human being. You can see the poor man's completely lost.'

'Is that my fault? I'm not responsible for the pitiful state he's in.'

'You are a little, actually. He needs help and you're content to just throw him a bone. Don't tell me you don't feel anything at all ...'

'A burning desire to show him the door with my foot up his backside, that's what I feel!'

'You're lying. You're as lost as he is. Anyone would think you're ashamed to take him in your arms.'

'You're totally mad. You read too many women's magazines. Paternal instinct, blood of my blood! It's all nonsense!'

'But look at yourself. You've changed since he's been here; you never take your eyes off him, as if you're looking for yourself in him.'

'For a mirror, one could do better. He's pathetic, a failure. And anyway, why are you interfering in the first place? What gives you the right to judge me?'

'I'm not judging you, I feel sorry for you. He may be a failure, as you say, but he's young, he still has his chances, while you …'

'What about me?'

'You must have made a mess of things in your life in order to have become what you are. Too bad. It's a waste.'

Thérèse turned on her heel and disappeared. Monsieur Lavenant felt an enormous weight descend on his shoulders. He was short of air like newborns who suffocate between two sobs. Anger and confusion created uncontrollable turbulence in his head. He felt like a boxer alone in a ring with no one to fight but himself. He looked around for something to break – it didn't matter what. He was about to grab the lamp on the little desk when he caught sight of the letter beginning 'My dear Thérèse …' All that emptiness, all that blank space that followed made him dizzy, forcing him to sit down. He couldn't take his eyes off the pure white page splashed with light from the lamp. Automatically, his right hand took hold of the pen: 'Well, yes, I have been a father for two days. I have a child but he is an orphan …'

When Thérèse and Jean-Baptiste came back they found him asleep, forehead resting on the desk, and the page completely filled with his small handwriting.

My dear Thérèse …

Well, yes, I have been a father for two days. I have a child but he is an orphan. It's rather unusual … but that's how it is. It has had the same effect on me as learning of my own death. He looks like me, it appears; personally I don't see it – he's much too young and I wouldn't wish that on him anyway. What would the world do with another Édouard Lavenant?

You know how old I am, my dear Thérèse. Who knows better than you my physical and mental decrepitude? I'm a wreck, aren't I? You may understand what it's like for me to feel this old wrinkled prune of a heart beat again in my hollow chest. I'm afraid of this new life; it's as though I had to start everything again from the beginning, question everything again, tear down the citadel of certainties in which I have taken refuge for so long. What an irony of fate to see the past resurface just as my memory is emptying like a basin of stale water. Thanks to you, I was gradually learning to accept this state of affairs serenely, aspiring to nothing more now than to live hour by hour, minute by minute, second by second. Old people, like lovers, are alone in the world, which is to say, profoundly egotistical. They need to be understood, they are fragile; with the slightest draught their bones shatter like glass. Everything is too strong for them, the cold, the heat; they protect themselves from life while they wait for death.

And then suddenly this vision of youth standing before me like a phantom ... Recognising this son meant looking myself in the face, and that is something which, through cowardice, I have always refused to do. With all the strength I have left I have fought against this unfamiliar emotion which has gripped me since Jean-Baptiste's arrival. Everything for which I reproached him was really addressed to myself. Now I surrender. I lower the arm which I raised against him and offer him my hand. I don't care what he may or may not have done, good or bad. Jean-Baptiste was born two days ago and that is all that matters. And in any case which of us has greater need of the other?

My dear Thérèse, will you help me in this task by assuming the place which falls to you at the core of this odd family? I wish it with all my heart.

Yours, Édouard

Jean-Baptiste handed the letter to Thérèse without meeting her gaze. The sheet was trembling in his hand. Thérèse folded it up carefully and slipped it into her pocket. After putting Monsieur Lavenant to bed they had each gone back to their own room but, unable to sleep, had met again in the early hours in the kitchen, where the remnants of night still stagnated.

'A little coffee?'

'Yes please.'

It was a day like any other except that it seemed to be setting in for eternity. Jean-Baptiste tilted his head back and gave his neck a rub.

'I think I'll go for a walk. I need to stretch my legs.'

When he had gone out, Thérèse set about removing all traces of the evening before, emptying the ashtrays, washing up, cleaning the floor, exorcism by housework. She felt no tiredness; floor cloth, broom and duster flew in her hands and her feet scarcely touched the floor. She made a mental note that the walls could do with a good lick of paint and it would be nice to change the sun-bleached curtains in the living room. Yellow perhaps, that would be more cheerful. Then in a short pause she dreamed of the little blue dress she had thought about buying on her last trip to the market. For lunch she would make a Swiss chard gratin, yes, a nice chard gratin with béchamel sauce. Édouard was wild about it. A mouse moving along the skirting board stopped just opposite her, staring at her with its little round eyes. Thérèse just shook her duster and the creature vanished into a tiny hole behind the sink.

Édouard had been awake for some time but couldn't manage to drag himself out of bed. Or rather he didn't want to. He didn't regret the letter he had written but dreaded coming face to face with Thérèse and Jean-Baptiste, which was unavoidable. Never had he felt this exposed, this unprotected; so much so that he thought he wouldn't ever get up, speak, eat or laugh again. The effort he'd had to put into writing those few sentences had drained him of all substance. Opening his eyes, he had been amazed that he was still alive. It was rather like a failed suicide. While he knew that this unpleasant sense of vulnerability was only the result of his wounded pride, he had enough of it left to refuse a complete surrender. His last trump cards lay in his age and the precariousness of his mental health. That was why he had let himself be carried like a parcel the previous evening when he could perfectly well have gone upstairs to bed on his own. After what he considered an exemplary *mea culpa*, the least they could do was be concerned about his condition, cosset him, do him justice and homage. Otherwise, of what possible use was redemption?

But his overfull bladder compelled him to get up, slip on

his dressing gown and make a rush for the toilet. No sooner had he got back into bed than there was a knock on the door and, without waiting for a reply, Thérèse appeared with the breakfast tray. The beatific smile on her face exasperated him in the extreme.

'I heard you going to the toilet and thought you'd like to have your breakfast in bed.'

His only answer was to turn his face to the wall.

'It's a fine day, a little wind but the weather's good. Shall I open the shutters? All right, I'll leave you then. Have you remembered we were going to see the vultures at the Rocher du Caire? The weather's ideal; it would be good to be there by about eleven. Édouard, are you listening to me? Édouard? Stop being so childish. No one's cross with you, quite the reverse. Don't spoil everything. Jean-Baptiste himself fetched the croissants; they're freshly baked. We'll wait for you. It's only half past nine, take your time. I'm so proud of you. What you did was very brave, worthy of a true father.'

Left on his own, Édouard pushed back the covers and punched open the shutters with his fist. The daylight was like a pail of water full in the face. 'It was very brave, worthy of a true father ... I'll say!' He wolfed down both croissants, drank his coffee in one go, showered and took an absolute age to get dressed, as if he were going out on a date. When he appeared before Thérèse and Jean-Baptiste he was wearing a pearl-grey pinstripe suit, a soft panama hat and was wreathed in clouds of vetiver.

'Well, what are we waiting for?'

This theatrical entrance left the other two speechless. All he needed now was a cane, which he naturally found in the umbrella stand, a metal-tipped walking stick with a handle shaped like a bulldog. He twirled it a few times, as if trying out the balance of a sword, then leaned on it, legs crossed and arching his eyebrows. He wasn't lacking in style but his bad night had given him a waxy complexion. He was like a waxwork from the Musée Grevin on a day off.

'Well then, are we off?'

'Of course.'

Édouard refused to get into the front of the car. 'At my age one sits in the back, leaving the risks to those with their whole lives ahead of them.' Thérèse drove carefully. Édouard talked constantly, about everything and nothing, like those who are uncomfortable with silence. It was only once they'd parked the car at the end of the little path and gone a hundred metres or so that the verbal diarrhoea stopped for lack of breath. Thérèse went in front, and Jean-Baptiste made clumsy attempts to match his stride to his father's.

'Are you all right?'

'Of course I'm all right!'

'You can lean on my arm if you like.'

'I have more trust in my stick. I'm fine I tell you, son.'

'Can I call you Papa?'

'Might as well. Tell me, what are you good at?'

'Well, er … not much. I studied accountancy.'

'And we've seen where that got you. Haven't you got a passion for something … I don't know, model-making, travel, watercolours?'

'I studied astrology in prison. I know how to do a birth chart.'

'That's a lot of good to us! An astrologer!'

'I'm not as stupid as all that, I'm a fast learner. Look.'

Jean-Baptiste stopped, stuck two fingers in his mouth and filled his lungs. He produced such a piercing whistle that a long way ahead, even with the wind against him, Thérèse turned round.

'Not bad.'

'I practised this morning. With the smoke rings I'm not quite there yet.'

'A whistling astrologer ... It's a start. Go on, give me your arm and take my stick – it's more of a nuisance to me.'

Thérèse had arrived at the top well before them. She had always been proud of her legs, not for their shapeliness but because they were strong and reliable, like a team of Percheron horses. They had never let her down. Leaning against the big wooden cross, shading her eyes with one hand, she followed the slow progress of father and son, arm in arm, on the path. From time to time they would pause. Édouard was holding his hat on and would nod his head as if affirming something. Jean-Baptiste signalled his agreement in the same way. Without knowing what they were talking about she sensed the two of them were getting along extremely well. Her heart was pounding in her chest, less from the physical effort than because she was certain she had finally attained the happiness she had been waiting for all her life. She smiled as the wind played around her like a young dog, blowing her hair back onto her cheeks and forcing her to hold her skirt down with one hand. The wood of the cross vibrated at her back. She turned round, eyes filled with tears: 'Make this last for ever ...'

'Something wrong, Thérèse? Do you feel dizzy?'

With their jacket tails flapping around them, the two men looked like birds about to take flight.

'No, it's the wind.'

'It's mighty strong, that's for sure. Oh, Jean-Baptiste, look, there they are!'

Two vultures launched themselves a few metres away,

regal, their outspread wings sweeping through space, eyes fixed, hooked beaks parting the sky like the prow of a boat. Three others followed, as if from nowhere, scratching cabbalistic signs on the azure expanse. Jean-Baptiste spread out his arms, facing into the wind, leaning at a 45-degree angle, mouth open, eyes closed.

'I spent hours staring at the window of my cell. "All that blue for nothing," I'd think. Eventually I no longer saw the wire netting, the bars … For a moment I was free.'

The wind had gone mad, intoxicated by the birds. It was making them draw incredible arabesques as if it wanted to prove to us poor earthbound creatures the eternal supremacy of the void.

'Hey, my hat!'

The white panama spun on the cliff edge and lodged in the branches of a bush lower down. Jean-Baptiste rushed over.

'Leave it, Jean-Baptiste, it's too windy – let it go!'

'It's not too far; I can reach.'

Thérèse and Édouard clutched each other. Pressed against the rock, clinging onto the stump of a thorny bush with one hand, Jean-Baptiste inched his other arm towards the hat. He finally managed to catch the brim between two fingers, and looked up at Thérèse and Édouard with a radiant smile.

'Got it!'

At that moment the root gave way. His smile froze and an astonished expression flicked his eyes wide open. Jean-Baptiste toppled backwards, hat in hand, like a music-hall entertainer taking his bows. His body plummeted some hundred metres onto a vulture's eyrie, from which the terrified female flew up with the shrillest of cries. Thérèse fell to her knees, arms hanging by her sides. Her lips were moving but no sound came out. The raptors were wheeling, undecided, up above the corpse which the sky had delivered to their door.

'It's not right, leaving him up there.'

'Why? Would you prefer it if he turned into a sack of maggots six feet underground?'

'I'm not saying that, but it's not Christian.'

'Big deal! In many countries no one would be shocked. It's clean, useful and spiritually impeccable.'

'Don't you feel any sorrow, Édouard?'

'What difference does it make what I feel? It's not me I'm thinking of but him. All his life he tried to take off, but, maybe because he didn't spread his wings wide enough, he never could. A few brief forays outside his feathered nest, stolen hopes, nothing more. Now he's soaring, he's in every one of those birds churning the sky. I'm certain that at last he feels at home. I'd rather think of Jean-Baptiste as I watch them wheeling freely in the boundless sky than when I'm staring at an icy marble slab. Besides, I would never have gone there, I've got a horror of graveyards – they smell of rotting geraniums and you get dodgy people there.'

'Well, personally I'll never be able to look at the creatures ever again. And you'll be bringing trouble to your door; it's against the law not to declare someone's death! You can be sure that sooner or later his body will be found ... What's left of him, rather – his clothes, watch, papers ... They'll suspect you of killing him, because no reasonable person would act the way you are. We've got to go to the police station; there's still time.'

'Do you think so?'

'I'm absolutely sure of it. Trust me, Édouard.'

Édouard had to admit that Thérèse was right, but he balked at the chore. They were going to have to explain the inexplicable, and he felt that was beyond him. He wasn't afraid, it was quite simply a nuisance.

'So we'll go then?'

'Purely to please you.'

The gendarmerie was no bigger than a family-size box of matches, covered in ochre rendering and topped by a dishcloth of a flag in mauve, beige and pink. The two gendarmes manning it were fine, but seemingly as deaf as each other; everything had to be repeated three or four times. Out of cowardice, Édouard had opted to play the senile old man, and it was Thérèse who answered the questions. The typewriter didn't work very well and there was a smell of sweat and stale cigarettes.

'But why wait so long before coming to make your statement?'

'Monsieur Lavenant felt unwell. I had to attend to him.'

'It's five o'clock already. My men are going to have difficulty recovering the body ... We'll come and pick you up in the morning for the identification.'

From trying not to hear anything, Édouard had a buzzing in his ears when they left, as if on a plane coming in to land after a long flight. They walked home. As they passed the bakery, Thérèse stopped to buy bread. On the glass door was a notice announcing a Mass on Saturday at 10 a.m. in memory of little Ange Spitallieri who had been killed in a tricycle accident.

They had dinner early, barely touching their soup and exchanging no more than two or three words. It was still light when they went up to bed, exhausted but sure they wouldn't be able to fall asleep any time soon. After tossing and turning a thousand times, Édouard got up and opened the window wide. The dark spread like an ink stain in the room.

'What does it all mean, all this dark, all this time?'

The quick padded steps of a cat on the tiles answered him, only to be snatched away again by the thick, echoless silence.

'Édouard? Who are you talking to?'

'Who d'you think I'd be talking to? Nobody.'

He came back and stretched out next to her, shivering, incapable of formulating the slightest thought, not that he had any.

'Can you hear, Thérèse?'

'What?'

'All this nothing, this emptiness surrounding us … I think we've been forgotten. Not a breath of wind, not a cat miaowing, not a rustling in the leaves … People have abandoned the world; there's only us left.'

'I can hear your heart beating.'

'It's just habit. It's striking its anvil like an old workman who doesn't know how to do anything else.'

'And my heart, can you hear it?'

'Yes, it's answering mine. It doesn't know why it's beating either. It's beating because it's been told to beat. Thérèse, will you suck me off?'

Thérèse gave a start beneath the sheet, a sort of gagging, but her hand gripped Édouard's shoulder more tightly.

'I'm sorry, Édouard. I don't think I can. I've never done it. It's not that it disgusts me, it's just that … I wouldn't know how to …'

'Don't apologise, I understand. To tell you the truth I don't really feel like it. I can't get to sleep so I just thought that maybe …'

'I can masturbate you if you want? I've already done that, to a man in the hospital. He had only a short time to live. The two of us struggled for quite a while. He didn't get there. I was doing my best though. No doubt I'm not cut out for that. He'd been very badly burned and it was the only part of his body that had been spared. He stroked my hair and, beneath the bandages covering his face, he smiled at me. He died two days later.'

Monsieur Lavenant propped himself up on one elbow and felt for his cigarettes. In the glow from the lighter flame he saw the mass of Thérèse's red hair spread out on the pillow, a sepia pool, an armful of floppy seaweed.

'As soon as we're finished with all this, we'll go away.'

'Where to?'

'I don't know. Wherever you want; go away just for the sake of it. Here isn't there, and you're bound to get there one day or another. Do you want to go back to Alsace?'

'I don't know. I've no family there, no ties. It was so long ago …'

'I said that off the top of my head, just to start us thinking; I could just as well have said Mont-Saint-Michel. What about abroad, does that appeal to you?'

'Isn't it a bit far?'

'That depends. Switzerland's next door. It's peaceful, Switzerland, and yet it's abroad.'

'Do you think I'd get used to it?'

'Of course, it's like here.'

'Then why go there?'

'Why? Why? Because it's like here only more expensive, that's why!'

'That's a stupid answer!'

'A stupid question deserves a stupid answer! You don't ask why people go to Switzerland, they just go, full stop, end of story.'

'No need to get angry! If that's what you want, we'll go to Switzerland.'

'My, oh, my … It takes you an age to make a decision. You'll like it, you'll see; it's very clean, the climate's good for you and although the clocks are always right, time passes more slowly there than anywhere else in the world. All old people like Switzerland.'

'Do you consider me old?'

'No, but that'll come soon enough. You'll be grateful to me when you're old in Switzerland. Now we have to sleep.'

The dark was no longer as dark. With the decision, a door had opened a crack, and behind it a vague glimmer could be seen, the germ of a future.

'Thérèse, I love falling asleep in your arms …'

The dawn had a muddy complexion. The sky was wondering about going off sick. It was a 'roll on bedtime' sort of a day. The two policemen from the previous afternoon seemed in a similar mood when they appeared at Monsieur Lavenant's door. As their van was too big to get along the narrow street, all four of them had to make their way back to it on foot, under the prurient eye of the neighbour spying on them from behind his curtains.

'Hey, Miriam, what did I say? Pretends to be a real gent, that one, and ends up flanked by policemen.'

Thérèse was white with shame as she got into the vehicle. Monsieur Lavenant just looked extremely weary. Two or three people on their way to empty their dustbins stared at them and whispered. Everyday people who today weren't everyday people any more. Édouard shrugged his shoulders.

'It's ridiculous, all this fuss and bother. We could have walked to the gendarmerie.'

'It's the rules, Monsieur.'

'Rules, bah!'

The garage adjacent to the police station, the place tyres were stored, was where Jean-Baptiste's body had been laid out, on a wooden board supported by two trestles. An ambulance was parked beside it. Two men in white coats stopped playing football with an old tennis ball when they arrived.

'We'll need to be quick as the ambulance has to get off to the morgue. It's not very savoury; the vultures didn't leave much. I don't know which of you …'

'Stay here, Thérèse, I'll go.'

The first thing Édouard noticed, even before the sheet was lifted, was that the loafer was missing from Jean-Baptiste's left foot.

The sock had been reduced to shreds of elastic thread at the ankle, and the foot to some bones held together by purplish tendons.

'Will you be all right?'

Édouard nodded his head. Of course he'd be all right. He had been born in Lyon, the home of the puppet Guignol – what was there to fear in a marionette without strings?

The teeth were immaculate and one of them, a gold molar, reflected the daylight's milky gleam. Jean-Baptiste was smiling because that's all a human being is left with once the skin and flesh are stripped away. All that remained of the eyes and nose – the tastiest morsels no doubt – were unfathomable cavities allowing you to imagine the vacuity of the skull, jaggedly split like a coconut shell and already orbited by a big fat fly. Lower down, the ribs protruded under the torn shirt and the entire entrails and internal organs had disappeared. A burst drum. The hands like small rusty tools were clutching nothingness. Two fingers were missing from the right hand and the thumb from the left. The rest was just shreds, leftovers from a banquet too soon interrupted by the rescuers' arrival. In spite of the products with which he had been sprayed, Jean-Baptiste was giving off a stench of flatulence.

'Do you recognise the victim?'

'The very image of his father.'

'What?'

'Sorry, yes, it's definitely him.'

The two men in white coats stowed Jean-Baptiste in the ambulance and Monsieur Lavenant, accompanied by the officer, rejoined Thérèse in the fetid offices of the gendarmerie. Once again it was necessary to go over the distressing banality of the previous day's events. They had to sign a statement and were asked to remain available to the authorities until the post-mortem. All these formalities were lengthy and boring; it was like being back at school. Monsieur Lavenant refused to let the police take them home.

'Thank you, you've done enough.'

They met no one on their way home, or else they didn't notice, each of them was so lost in their own thoughts. Édouard's naturally took him towards Switzerland. The page had been turned; soon he would no longer remember it. The next chapter opened with the Swiss flag, which had always made him think of an Elastoplast cross stuck over a red mouth. This symbol of mutism suited him perfectly. He had already left.

'Well?'

'Well what?'

'What was he like?'

'Dead.'

'Yes, but …'

'Dead like a dead man, out of his body. Only the shell of him was there.'

'You're speaking about him as if he were a thing!'

'Well, yes, a still life. There's no reason to be offended by it. Oh, it's raining … You didn't bring an umbrella, obviously. What were you thinking of, Thérèse?'

Despite hurrying they arrived home soaking wet. Édouard lit a fire and Thérèse made tea. It was barely eleven o'clock but you would have thought it was the evening. Édouard was delighted. If only every day could be this short. Twenty-four hours, that's far too many! Half would be enough, eight for sleeping, four for getting bored stiff. Twelve hours gone to waste when they could be useful to someone else, a poor man for example. What a gift that would be!

The log that Édouard was poking at in the fire had taken on the appearance of a bison's head, blowing jets of spitting flames out of every orifice: flaring nostrils, hollow eye sockets, misshapen ears. Paradoxically the more the piece of wood was consumed, the more alive it became. It was fascinating.

'Stop poking at that log, Édouard. You'll end up setting light to the house.'

'Bah, what does it matter, we're never coming back.'

'We can't leave nothing but ashes behind us.'

The button Thérèse was sewing on slipped out of her hands, rolled over the stone slabs, and settled again, spinning like a top between her feet, almost back where it had started. They had both followed its spiral course and were now staring at it, a mother-of-pearl button with four holes in it. It looked like the world's navel.

After several days the authorities had to acknowledge that Jean-Baptiste's death was simply the result of an accidental fall, even if the victim's dubious past and his uncertain relations with Monsieur Lavenant allowed some doubt to remain. At any rate the latter was now free to go wherever he wanted.

They left one morning, early. The previous day Thérèse had cleaned the house from top to bottom. No trace of their presence remained, and Thérèse was disturbed by this as she glanced round for the last time before closing the door. Who could have imagined that people had prepared snails and lit a fire in the grate here, that they had laughed, cried, loved and suffered … The smell of the cleaning products had left a whiff of amnesia. Thérèse felt tears come to her eyes.

'What's wrong?'

'It's as if nothing had ever been …'

'Well, yes, it's as if … that's how it is. You wipe everything away and start again; life is a palimpsest. Oh, look where you're going, Thérèse, or you'll miss the step.'

'What shall I do with the keys?'

'I don't know … Hang them on the nail under the beam.

Whoever finds them can have them, the rust first and foremost.'

It had been agreed that they would spend a day or two in Lyon, just while Monsieur Lavenant sorted out some business. Thérèse's old car struggled and coughed its way along under the weight of luggage.

'First thing tomorrow we'll buy a new one. We can't go to Switzerland in an old jalopy like this, people would take us for gypsies.'

'She's still game! She's overloaded, that's all. I couldn't bear to see her go to the scrapyard.'

'We'll put her in my garage then. She's earned her retirement, don't you think? What are you looking at in the mirror?'

'I thought I saw two women waving us off at the corner of the street.'

'One tall and one small?'

'Yes. Do you know them?'

'Vaguely. I've seen them go by.'

The sky was as white and opaque as a cinema screen. It seemed as if at any minute Charlie Chaplin would appear, twirling his cane, on the horizon of the motorway. Thérèse kept to the slow lane, huddled over the steering wheel, stoically putting up with the exhaust fumes from the lorries she couldn't bring herself to overtake. Every time she went under a bridge she would shut her eyes, her lips stammering out unintelligible prayers.

'Open your eyes, for God's sake! You'll have us off the road.'

'I can't help it, I hate the motorway, especially the bridges. There's always people on them looking at us.'

'So?'

'I'm scared they'll throw things at us.'

'That's ridiculous! What do you think they'd throw at us?'

'I don't know … A bicycle, a log, stones … It *has* happened.'

'I love travelling with you. It feels so safe. You can stop at the next service station; I urgently need to go.'

Hemmed in by two articulated lorries, Thérèse missed the first one. Édouard's bladder was at bursting point when they came to the second. He rushed into the toilets, the ones for disabled people which he found more spacious, and stayed there for some time, prostate oblige. It was like the North Pole, a vast expanse of pristine tiling, from which seals, penguins and bears might be expected to appear.

Thérèse was waiting for him in front of the coffee machines. They each had a tomato consommé. In the nine hours since they had left, they had covered only about a hundred kilometres. Tousled kids, bright red in the face, were clamouring loudly for everything the service station had to offer them: cuddly monkeys, cakes, fizzy drinks, key rings, music cassettes, sandwiches, regional specialities, knives … To relax after long hours at the wheel, fathers were practising virtual steering on video screens. It was a strange, murky world, slightly resembling that of a Jacques Cousteau documentary. They left their cups still half full on some plastic mushrooms and took refuge in their car, certain of having narrowly escaped some sort of danger.

They took over four hours to reach the capital of the Gauls. Terrified by the traffic, Thérèse got lost a thousand times before – nerves in shreds and totally distraught – drawing up in front of Monsieur Lavenant's residence in Boulevard des Belges, a stone's throw from the sparkling gates of Parc de la Tête d'Or.

The apartment was immense, seven rooms, maybe more, stretching over almost five hundred square metres and with very high ceilings. Édouard showed Thérèse round at top speed before abandoning her in the drawing room while he shut himself in his study to make some urgent phone calls.

Perched gingerly on the edge of a sofa made of the thickest leather, Thérèse looked over the decor surrounding her. It was expensive, to be sure; each piece of furniture, every carpet and ornament had to be worth a small fortune, but this ostentatious luxury dripping with gold and satin was out of keeping with Monsieur Lavenant's character. It was hard to picture him moving around in this monstrous bonbonnière in which the sugared almond-coloured lampshade frills vied for first prize in the bad-taste stakes with the chantilly cream tie-backs for the fuchsia curtains. The plethora of objects in the display cases, on the occasional tables and on the shelves was enough to give you indigestion. In a vain attempt to find a moment's escape from the riot of bronze, porcelain and other biscuit ware, Thérèse's eyes lit on one of the countless terrible paintings staining the walls. Like the others it depicted a bunch of flowers, but the artist had larded it with so much red and blue that it had the same effect as an open abdomen spewing its steaming entrails. Thérèse found refuge only in contemplating a triangle of sky which gave the window a matt-white tint.

'Say what you like, people are not like us.'

So this was how other people lived. Well, so long as they liked it …

She got no further in her reflections. Édouard had joined her, a leather briefcase under his arm, bouncing with energy.

'Right, a car's coming for me. I've two or three matters to sort out. Make yourself at home. I'll be back around eight. I'll book a table at Orsi's, very nearby; that'll be simpler for this evening … Sorry?'

'I didn't say anything.'

'Oh, I thought … Right, well …'

Édouard seemed like a different person in these surroundings, smaller somehow. He was like one of those portraits of adolescents you find when leafing through a family album, awkward-looking, ill at ease.

'Cécile had terrible taste. See you this evening.'

When he returned shortly before eight o'clock, Thérèse was still in the same place. Only the now open window showed that she had moved. The sun was sinking behind Fourvière hill.

Édouard talked and talked, of things Thérèse understood absolutely nothing about: his business, his lawyer, figures. She wasn't listening to him in any case; all her attention was focused on the excellent blanquette d'écrevisses au vin jaune which she was savouring in tiny mouthfuls.

'It's atrocious, Thérèse, isn't it?'

'Sorry, what's atrocious?'

'My place, it's atrocious, don't you think?'

'I wouldn't say that. It's … big.'

'I'm going to throw all that out. Every day she would bring home some thing or other, some whatnot, so hideous that I always used to wonder where on earth would sell it.'

'You know, tastes and colours …'

'No! It wasn't that she had bad taste, she had none at all. She didn't respond to colours or flavours or … Take your blanquette, for example. You've savoured it. Well, she'd have swallowed it like a mess of tapioca. Imagine a bell with absolutely no resonance. She was extraordinary, unfathomably vacuous. It was no doubt to fill that void that she bought all that, to please me, maybe … Or to annoy me; I've never known which. On the other hand she could do impeccable imitations of farm animals.'

'Farm animals?'

'Yes, cows, cockerels, goats, sheep … You couldn't tell them from the real thing. She could have had a career in music hall. Animals would answer her, you know. She could hold a conversation with a duck for nearly forty minutes!'

'She loved animals.'

'I don't think so. It always ended in a row. They'd try to bite her and she'd hit them with a stick. She knew their languages, that was all. A pointless gift, like her beauty. She never made use of it. I got to wishing that she would cheat on me. She had many admirers. It never happened.'

Thérèse noticed something like a little wave in Édouard's look, with a mast in the distance, sinking beneath the foam.

'Is something wrong? You haven't touched your plate.'

'I'm fine. It's strange, I can't remember her face at all, only her voice ...'

On leaving Orsi's, Édouard went in the opposite direction to the one from which they had arrived. Thérèse was surprised but, not knowing the city, followed him. After a good quarter of an hour (whereas they'd taken only five or six minutes to walk to the restaurant from Édouard's apartment) she asked him where they were going.

'I've no idea, I'm following you.'

'But we're going to your apartment!'

'Oh ...'

'Your place, Boulevard des Belges.'

'Boulevard des Belges ...'

'Don't you remember where you live?'

'No.'

'The big apartment that's ... ugly.'

They had taken so many turnings down so many empty, identical streets that Thérèse now had no idea at all where they were. Luckily a passer-by pointed them in the right direction. They had gone a long way off course but Édouard seemed unconcerned. He let himself be guided by Thérèse with the serene confidence a blind man has in his dog. Finally she recognised the façade and the carriage entrance opposite the park gates. Access was by a numerical code.

'Seven, eight, nine, three.'

'You're sure?'

'Of course!'

Thérèse pressed the buttons without really believing him, yet the gate opened straight away.

'Are you making fun of me?'

'Why?'

'You don't know where you live but you can remember the code?'

'Get in quickly instead of asking stupid questions. It's starting to rain.'

Édouard was sitting in a chair, his morocco-leather briefcase flat on his knees. He was wearing a dark suit, white shirt, red tie and black shoes. There was a strong smell of aftershave emanating from him. Like a traveller on a station platform, he was waiting. For what? He would have found it very difficult to say. He knew only that he had to wait. Outside it was still dark. The 100 watts pouring from an imitation Venetian chandelier lit him cruelly but he seemed scarcely to notice. With age you become patient, giving time no more value than it deserves; you put it in your pocket with your handkerchief on top and take tiny sips of the present like a glass of port. Oh yes, of course! It was coming back to him. He was waiting for his driver, who was to take him to Maître Billard, his lawyer's. Smiling, he tapped his briefcase. Everything was there, neatly arranged. Half of his possessions would go to Thérèse, the other half to Jean-Baptiste. The split seemed equitable. One person would be able to live out her days in peace and the other finally to embark on a life worthy of the name. You had to know how to wipe the slate clean. Which young man has never done anything stupid? Besides, there were mitigating circumstances. An orphan, a

119

child who'd been given life without an instruction manual. He was entitled to a second chance. It was for him, Édouard Lavenant, to give him that and he felt great pride and a profound relief. No one would be able to reproach him for being a bad father, no one …

He thumped his fist on the table and a silver saucer flew across the room before landing, spinning, on the marble floor of the entranceway. The cymbal clash spread in concentric waves throughout the house.

Thérèse appeared, hair untidy, rubbing her eyes, one heavy breast escaping from her dressing gown, pulled on in a hurry.

'Whatever are you doing here?'

'Waiting for my driver. I've got an appointment with Maître Billard.'

'It's five o'clock in the morning!'

'Oh …'

'You need to go back to bed.'

'But I've been to sleep, I'm dressed …'

'It's too early, Édouard. Come on, I'll help you.'

Once undressed he'd fallen asleep again immediately. Thérèse, on the other hand, lying next to him, found it impossible to go back to sleep. She was suffocating in this house with its clutter of hostile objects which, every time she moved, immediately seemed to gather together to block her way. Unable to bear it any longer, she got up and opened the window wide, in desperate need of air. The fluffy foliage of the unnaturally green plane trees stretched, dripping, the whole length of the avenue. On the pavement opposite, two women hurried past, clutching an umbrella. The smaller of the two looked up at the window and for a split second her glasses captured the street lamp's gleam. Thérèse recoiled. She could have sworn the woman had given her a slight nod.

Thérèse was waiting for Édouard in one of those imposing brasseries in Place Bellecour which make you feel as if you've gone back a hundred years: lofty ceilings, over-ornate mouldings, murals with pastoral scenes in pastel colours, gleaming brass, polished wood, waiters with long white aprons and handlebar moustaches. The clientele was in keeping. Beyond the window the square with its brick-red ground made you think of an enormous tennis court, with the equestrian statue of Louis XIV as an incongruous centrepiece. It would no doubt be hot today. Mist was rising from the freshly watered pavements, with a smell of hot damp cloth.

She had woken Édouard at eight o'clock. He had no memory of having been awake earlier, but as he seemed in a particularly good mood Thérèse hadn't mentioned it. After breakfast he had insisted she accompany him, something she had gladly agreed to (any excuse to get out of the house) while refusing to go up to the offices out of decency. She wouldn't want people to think …

All this seemed slightly mad, illogical, but Édouard's enthusiasm was so infectious that she felt ready to follow him to the ends of the earth, all the more so as this would probably be no further away than Lake Geneva. She didn't care about the distance; for once she was resolved to take a train that was going somewhere. Édouard needed her, more today than yesterday perhaps.

She saw him go past the café so quickly she had no time to knock on the window. Then he reappeared, going in the opposite direction in just as much of a hurry, talking to himself and shaking his head. Suddenly, instead of coming into the café, he crossed the road, paying no attention to the cars screeching to a halt in front of him, walked across the square and began going round and round the statue. Thérèse paid for her drink and rushed over to join him.

'Now, Thérèse, what have you been doing? Our plane leaves in two hours; we're cutting it fine.'

'Two hours? What about our luggage?'

'We'll buy everything once we're there. You've needed a new wardrobe since birth. Taxi!'

Satolas Airport had been rechristened Saint-Exupéry and no one had informed Monsieur Lavenant.

'Saint-Ex! What a name. Saint-Ex! Well, if that's progress ...'

The car smelled of new plastic. An unidentifiable orange furry creature was bouncing on a length of elastic beneath the rear-view mirror.

'Couldn't you take that thing down, it's getting annoying ...'

'No, M'sieur. It was a gift from my children.'

'Well, at least switch off the radio!'

'Yes, M'sieur.'

'Right, my secretary has booked us a hotel in Geneva. We'll hire a car locally and then we'll look for a chalet higher up in the mountains. Oh, Thérèse … Old age! That poor Billard is going completely gaga, yet he's ten years younger than me. I had to repeat things ten times for him and he kept replying, "Are you really sure, Édouard? Really sure?" It's terrible to see someone I've been friends with for thirty years in that state. But now everything's arranged. It was time Jean-Baptiste took over!'

'Jean-Baptiste?'

'Of course Jean-Baptiste. Until there's proof to the contrary, he's my only son!'

'But Édouard …'

'What?'

'Jean-Baptiste is dead!'

Édouard's face froze. His lower lip began to quiver and his eyes to blur. He turned his head towards the flat-roofed buildings with signboards on top which lined the road.

'Don't ever say that again, Thérèse.'

His good hand reached for Thérèse's and she took it. It was dry and cold, perhaps because of the air conditioning.

Thérèse had never travelled by plane. Airports were not like railway stations. Everything was cleaner, well looked after, hushed voices, a sort of hospital where people would just disappear without a trace, never die. Paradise was within arm's reach, no doubt because of the proximity of the sky. While waiting for Édouard, who had gone off somewhere, Thérèse watched the planes taking off for Bangkok, Rio de Janeiro, Toulouse, Milan, Lille, Strasbourg … The people you came across here weren't the same as those in the street. They smelled of elsewhere, wore different clothes, walked differently – more slowly, as if weightless. Here nothing was far away so you didn't hurry.

'Here, Thérèse, this is for you.'

Édouard was holding out a small bag embossed with the logo of a famous parfumier.

'You can open it on the plane. Let's hurry.'

Later, while Édouard was asleep with his head on her shoulder, she opened the package. It was a star-shaped bottle, filled with blue perfume. She sprayed a little on the back of her hand. It smelled of altitude, the blue sky above the clouds, a landscape she was discovering for the first time in her life.

'What are you doing, Thérèse?'

'Er … I'm making the bed.'

'You're making the bed. Would you like to do the washing up as well, while you're about it? Let me remind you that we're in one of the most opulent hotels in Geneva.'

Thérèse blushed. She hadn't been able to resist. She liked making the bed in the morning and to tell the truth she wouldn't have objected to the washing up either. Having been up since six, after washing and dressing as unobtrusively as possible she'd had nothing else to do, and ensconced herself on the balcony between two big ornamental vases, eventually feeling like one of them herself, until room service had arrived with breakfast.

'Leave it, I'll see to it. Monsieur is still asleep.'

The waiter, accustomed to fantasies of love affairs with servants, had given her a conspiratorial wink, which shocked her deeply.

'I'm sorry, Édouard. I can't just do nothing. It makes me feel …'

'Helpless?'

'A bit.'

'Wealth always does that to begin with, and then you get used to it.'

'I don't think I will.'

'Now put your jacket on, we're going out. You want things to do, you shall have them.'

The morning's shopping was a veritable Way of the Cross for Thérèse. They visited an incredible number of boutiques, each more luxurious than the last, and each time Thérèse came away more humiliated. As soon as she entered, even the most junior salesgirl would look her up and down, shooting her a contemptuous glance which made her even more gauche, stupid and inarticulate. She felt dirty, ugly and out of place, and if Édouard had not made all the decisions for her she would, from shame, have rushed to throw herself in the lake with a stone around her neck.

'Well, Thérèse, do you like this dress? Would you like to try another size?'

'No, no, it's fine.'

In the intimacy of the final fitting-room cubicle she dissolved into tears before her grotesque reflection. Never had she felt so miserable.

'Right, now you need a handbag. Hermès is just next door.'

'Please, Édouard, I'd like to go back to the hotel. I don't feel well.'

'Already? True, it's nearly one o'clock. Let's go for lunch. We still have the whole afternoon ahead of us.'

It was nice on the terrace. There was a cool breeze from the lake. The fillets of perch were excellent, the service impeccable, yet it was as if something like an imperceptible odour of putrefaction hung over this perfect world, accompanied by a worrying ticking sound. It was probably coming from Lake Geneva, the dull beat of an army on the march. It was as if all the clocks and all the watches had agreed to start an inexorable countdown which made you await with terror the imminent alarm bell announcing the attack.

'Dessert?'

'No! Thank you. Excuse me, Édouard, I don't feel very well. I'm going back to our room.'

'Do. I'll join you in a minute.'

Thérèse made her way unsteadily across the restaurant terrace, among the mummies with their clinking jewellery and shrill laughter, their skeletons jerking like miserable puppets. Their plasterwork make-up was flaking off, and underneath there was nothing, nothing but dry, white bone.

The room was littered with the packages Édouard had had delivered. It looked like Christmas gone wrong. She collapsed onto the bed and took refuge in sleep, her cheeks glazed with tears, the source of which she would have been unable to identify.

Tiny white yachts were racing one another on the blue waters of the lake, delicate angel feathers scattered by the whistle of a ferry as it returned to the landing stage. On the right, the proud water jet plumed over the city, lending an iridescence to the view of the mountains, but Monsieur Lavenant only had eyes for the magnificent pair of yellow Westons he had bought himself. Squeezed into the cane armchair on the balcony, legs outstretched, he banged them together. They reminded him of a pair of ducks. He would probably never wear them. They were simply beautiful, like Cécile ... He had wanted her and he had got her, solely for the pleasure of snaffling her from the pack of suitors who trailed after her with their tongues hanging out. It was as stupid as that. Cécile was a two-way mirror through which he could enjoy the ever-recurring spectacle of others' covetousness, of the thousand and one base deeds motivated by the desire to possess what one hasn't got. If they had only known, poor things ...

Monsieur Lavenant glanced over his shoulder. Thérèse was still asleep, one hand beneath her cheek, her presence confirmed by gentle snoring. It was reassuring.

'I could get some bread while I'm about it …' Édouard couldn't get the little phrase overheard in the street that morning out of his head. A man talking to himself outside a bakery. A phrase necessitating no metaphysical dissection, but which, unlike the many others one feels compelled to fill with sense, had the merit of saying what it meant. "I wasn't thinking of it, but since I have no bread left and I'm outside a bakery, I might as well get some bread." Contained in these simple words was all the good sense of humankind, which ensures we are still alive, standing, humble and irrefutable. The same good sense, no doubt, which had moved Thérèse to make the bed.

Make your bed and lie in it.

Ill-gotten gains profit no one.

Once a thief …

Slow and steady …

The pitcher goes to the well so often …

A never-ending list of ridiculous proverbs appeared before his eyes, like driving-school slides showing improbable scenarios.

'I've had it up to here with good sense! What the hell's she doing – is she dead or something?'

He flushed the loo several times without closing the door. Thérèse raised one eyelid, like a monitor lizard.

'What time is it?'

'Time to go for an ice cream.'

Her new natural-linen dress let the air through so deliciously that Thérèse blushed, as if she were out walking naked. By contrast, the too tight straps of her gold sandals were cruelly wounding her swollen feet. Édouard was wearing a suit that matched her dress and his yellow shoes captured the sun's rays beautifully. The two were like a team of horses. A couple of sickly-looking joggers in matching tracksuits ran past them, each on the verge of a heart attack.

'Have you noticed that old couples dress the same? Such a lack of taste!'

Quai Wilson, Quai du Mont-Blanc ... To rest their feet, which were killing them though they didn't say anything to each other, they stopped for a moment in front of the statue of Empress Sissi, sited at the spot where she is supposed to have been stabbed by an Italian anarchist. Thérèse found it disappointing.

'She doesn't look like Romy Schneider.'

And in fact the unpleasant bronze sculpture was more reminiscent of the horrible bunches of gladioli people give their mothers-in-law at Sunday lunchtimes than of the legendary actress's graceful outline.

'Do you know, she didn't notice anything at the time, a punch at most. She and her lady-in-waiting got into the boat and it was only in the cabin that she knew she was mortally wounded. How many of us are in that same situation, believing they're still alive when they're dead? It's a mystery. One acts as if ... And it works!'

They chose to have their ice cream at the Bains des Pâquis, a bathing place created by building out into the lake. Access was by a raised wooden walkway which gave you the impression of stepping onto the deck of a ship. The architecture of the rows of changing cubicles separated by duckboard pathways must have dated from the early twentieth century. It exuded an old-fashioned charm which the reggae music coming from the bar could not dispel.

The naked bodies of young Adonises glistening with sun-tan oil mingled uninhibitedly with the three-piece suits of respectable bankers, and mothers chasing after their shrieking offspring. Some were cruising, others having tea in the most civilised manner. Thérèse and Monsieur Lavenant took the table furthest from the bar, because of the music.

'This need for music all the time is crazy! It's everywhere: in shops, in the street, even in the hotel toilets! What's so frightening about silence?'

They ordered ice creams with exotic names, which turned out just to be scoops of vanilla and chocolate hidden under a layer of grated coconut. Opposite them, imperturbable, the water jet kept up its insolent ejaculation. Out of the corner of her eye, while she sucked her spoon, Thérèse stole furtive glimpses at the perfectly tanned youths brushing against each other suggestively, without eliciting the slightest disapproval from the worthy citizens.

'Honestly, really …'

'Honestly what?'

'But … See for yourself!'

'What is there to see?'

'Those youths there … they're that way inclined … In front of all those children. Honestly …'

'What's it to you? At least that lot don't reproduce, that's something. Tomorrow we'll begin our search for a chalet to rent, as high up and remote as possible.'

'Oh yes! I admit I feel out of place here. Édouard?'

'What?'

'There's a man looking at you very intently.'

'A man? Where?'

'Over there, leaning on the bar. It's funny … he could be you … He's coming over!'

Against the light Édouard could not make out the man's features, but the silhouette seemed familiar.

'Excuse me, are you by any chance Édouard Lavenant?'

Now the man was leaning over the table, his face appeared as plainly as his own reflection in a mirror. Except for the moustache, the close-cut hair, that sallow complexion and eyes with dark rings like two holes in an old pair of socks, this was his 'certified copy'.

'Jean!'

'Yes. Allow me to sit down – this is quite a shock. Forgive me, Madame, I haven't introduced myself. Jean Marissal, a very, very old friend of Édouard's. If I'd thought …'

Thérèse had heard it said that everyone on earth has a double, but that two of them should be intimately acquainted seemed almost miraculous.

'How did you recognise me after so many years?'

'Oh come, Édouard, how could I fail to recognise my own face?'

'Of course, that was stupid …'

It was when they had started their first year at the Lycée

du Parc in Lyon that they had discovered this odd whim of nature. Although their surnames differed the teacher had seated them side by side like twins. Other than this incredible physical resemblance, however, they differed in every respect. Édouard came from what is known in Lyon as the hill that prays, Fourvières, and Jean from the hill that works, Croix-Rousse. Édouard was as reserved and studious a child as Jean was exuberant and mischievous, attracting attention from those around him wherever he went. Right from the start Édouard suffered horribly from the existence of his double, but Jean very quickly grasped the benefits to be gained from their extraordinary likeness. For over a year Édouard had, like Dr Jekyll, to put up with the dire consequences of Mr Hyde's misdeeds. It was during a science lesson where they were dissecting frogs that Édouard put an end to this unjust fate by gashing Jean's cheek with a scalpel. The punishment was severe but he accepted it unflinchingly, even with relief. Henceforth, no matter what happened, people would always be able to tell them apart. From that moment, Jean's attitude towards him changed radically, resulting not in a real friendship but in a sort of complicity which made them respect each other. They were nicknamed 'the Duellists'. Then when they reached adulthood life took them in different directions. Édouard carried on his father's business and Jean embarked on a career as an artist. They had never seen each other again. With the tip of his finger, Jean stroked his scar, almost invisible now, masked by wrinkles.

'I daren't count the years.'

'No point. What are you doing here?'

'It's a meeting place – as you can see. I lived in Morocco for a long time but the climate no longer suited my health. Since I work with galleries in Geneva, Basle and Lausanne, I settled here.'

'Are you still painting?'

'Let's say I exist now only by virtue of having existed. What about you? Are you here on business?'

'No, it's out of my hands now; that's the right expression for it!' Édouard raised his crippled arm, letting it fall back onto the table. 'A stroke, several months ago.'

'So you're here to convalesce, as it were.'

'You could say that.'

A young man with curly hair and eyes like a gazelle, dressed in a tight-fitting black T-shirt, laid his hand on Jean's shoulder and whispered a few words in his ear.

'No, not tonight, Mehdi. Another time. Yes, I'll call you. Where are you staying?'

'At the Bristol, but we won't be there for long. I'd like to rent a house far away from it all; I need quiet.'

'I know of some. I live right up in the mountains, half an hour from the city. Speaking of which, what are you doing this evening?'

'Nothing special.'

'Then why not come over? I've got a splendid view over the lake, and I'll bring you back after dinner. It will give me a chance to get to know Madame. You'll have to excuse us, this meeting was so unexpected …'

'Not at all, I quite understand. We'd love to. What do you think, Édouard?'

'Why not?'

Thérèse had insisted on getting into the back, to give the two men a chance to reminisce, but neither of them seemed to want to take advantage of it. No doubt they needed some time to start up the time machine. The road looped round and sometimes your view plunged down to the mist-covered lake, sometimes your gaze came up against a phalanx of black pointed fir trees against a reddening sky.

The chalet was built on a rocky cliff, almost balancing on the top. A gap in the forest opened up a clear view over the lake; all that was visible of the opposite side were glimmering lights like fireflies, beyond which nothing else seemed real. Leaning on the balcony rail, Thérèse and Édouard silently drank in the peace of this majestic spectacle, which reminded them somewhat of the Rocher du Caire.

'This is exactly what we're looking for, a real eagle's nest.'

'You don't know how true that is. There are lots of them here. I spend hours watching them circling in the sky. Would you like a drink?'

Resinous scents wafted in through the wide-open picture window like incense. The living room where they drank champagne was vast and practically empty, minimally furnished with a table, sofa and, at the back of the room, a desk flanked by an armchair. Nothing on the walls, not one picture. The sole item of decoration was a sort of bronze wading bird some fifty centimetres tall, in a niche behind the sofa. It looked like a house someone was about to leave or had just moved into.

'It's a little bare but I love the space. I never have visitors. Before, I used to love objects. My house in Morocco was a veritable souk. I left everything behind. You change. With time, you prefer travelling light.'

'And it's easier to look after.'

'Exactly. You're quite right, Madame.'

Jean and Thérèse argued politely over who should make the dinner, and Thérèse won. Wouldn't you expect two old friends to have some time on their own? But above all she felt an overwhelming need to be in a kitchen again, to handle pans, plates, cutlery and glasses, things she understood, which understood her and which she had missed dreadfully since their departure from Rémuzat. She had a connoisseur's appreciation for the cleanliness of the place, the simplicity and quality of the utensils and the practicality of the way things were arranged. It was surprising for a bachelor. Jean showed her where to find everything she might need and in less than five minutes she was going backwards and forwards between oven and fridge, as much at home as a goldfish in its bowl. She threw herself into making a rice salad with tuna.

It was a house like this that they needed, quiet, far away from everything, with, if possible, this magnificent view, which at every hour of the day would remind them of the peace and sweetness of life. She would furnish it differently, of course. You could bring a little more warmth to the pretty chalet: carpets, curtains, these little nothings which mean everything. Aside from his manner, which was rather precious for a man, Jean was a charming person, attentive, delicate. A little too much so. When he smiled, and he smiled often, there was an air of melancholy about him which made you want to throw yourself out of the window. Men on their own … If they could find a similar house somewhere nearby, Édouard and he would be able to see each other, exchange ideas, talk about the good old days. It would do them good … The sound of the timer dragged her from her daydreams; the eggs were done.

To be honest, Édouard was no keener than Jean was to bring up the good old days. What preoccupied them, though they didn't mention it even as they stole glances at each other, was not this chance present but their future, as brief as it was uncertain. Jean emptied the last of the bottle into their champagne glasses, before sliding a silver powder compact out of the coffee-table drawer.

'May I?'

It was filled with white powder. Using a razor blade, he made a line of it on the mirror on the inside of the lid and then inhaled it through a straw.

'Are you taking drugs?'

'I'm anaesthetising myself. Does that shock you?'

'No. At our age we all have our drugs.'

'Thérèse?'

'Thérèse isn't a drug.'

'Forgive me. She's charming, very ... unspoilt. From you, that astounds me. You were always keener on women who enhanced your worth.'

'Maybe I'm not worth much any more. You live here alone then?'

'Solitary as a monk. When I have needs I go to the Bains des Pâquis, but that's less and less often now. I hadn't set foot there for six months. I was about to leave when I noticed you.'

'Aren't you afraid of problems?'

'What sort of problems? Oh, the powder, the boys? What do you think could happen to me now? Besides, this is Switzerland. If you have a bank account and make sure to cross at the crossing everything's allowed. Besides ... whatever I do I'm not risking a life sentence. You've seen the way I look, I'm already a condemned man. It's only a matter of days, hours ... I'm not even seeing my doctor any longer.'

'Are you frightened?'

'No, not really. It's a bit drawn out ...'

'And the painting?'

'I gave up a long time ago. You know, I've never been a great painter, an artist. I'm much too cowardly for that. Skilled technically, no more than that; bogged down in formal beauty, and charm. I painted portraits my whole life without realising that, contrary to appearances, behind every man and every woman there was a human being. But tell me, what are you in search of here?'

'Another life.'

Jean's face lit up like a lantern and he started laughing, which almost choked him.

'Another life? Is that all? At your age, aren't you ashamed? Wasn't your own enough for you?'

'That wasn't my life. I'm firmly convinced it was a mistake. Anyway, I've hardly any of it left; I've erased it all. Apart from this arm, which I don't miss, I'm in excellent health and ready to start all over again.'

Jean appeared to be weighing him up like some curious object found in a junk shop.

'I believe you could ... Why not? You've no children?'

'What for?'

'True, what for? They're no use; people like us have no need to live on. And yet, sometimes, without intending to, you know, like with plants, you end up producing offshoots.'

'I've never had green fingers. I've killed artificial flowers before now.'

'You always were a dried-up old stick.'

'So? The desert's dry but that doesn't stop it being alive.'

'And going on and on for ever ... I know a bit about that, I've done it enough. All the same, Switzerland, for two old sods like us ...'

Jean's laughter was as false as his teeth. Between the two men was everything that separates the beginning from the end, an uncertain and illusive no man's land. Jean lay back on the sofa cushions, eyes closed and hands behind his head.

'One day – I must have been eighteen – my father asked me, "What are you going to do with your life?" I had no answer for him. And today if I ask myself what I've done with my life, I'm just as mute. What happened in the meantime?'

Dinner was light-hearted and convivial. In earlier days Jean had liked cooking. Thérèse and he exchanged recipes, tagine with prunes for blanquette à l'ancienne. The wine was excellent. Édouard rather overdid it so that by the cheese course he was beginning to nod into his plate. Only snatches of conversation reached him now, or even just words like *ksar*, *moucharabieh*, *medina* with which Jean spiced the stories of his travels. Occasionally, after a juicy anecdote, Thérèse's laugh made him jump before he sank back into the sweet torpor of a child who falls asleep at the table.

'Édouard? ... Édouard? I can't wake him. I'm embarrassed; he's not used to drinking so much.'

'Let him sleep then. There's a guest room. You can spend the night here and I'll take you back tomorrow morning.'

'But what if he wakes up ... He'll be completely lost. Since his stroke his mind has gone blank at times ...'

'Don't worry about it. I'm an insomniac. You go to bed. I'll stay here beside him. When he wakes up I'll be with him.'

'That's very kind. It's awful, he won't accept ...'

'Being his age? Me neither. Don't worry about anything. The bedroom's at the end of the corridor, on the right, next to the bathroom. I've had a lovely evening.'

'So have I. Don't hesitate to ...'

'Goodnight.'

'"*Le héron au long bec emmanché d'un long cou* …" Well, Lavenant, I'm waiting for the next line – haven't you learned the text by heart? "The heron with a long beak …"'

Behind the sofa, the bronze bird was pointing its long sharp beak at Édouard. On each side its glass-paste eyes were peering into the darkness. Someone was murmuring at the other end of the room. Édouard propped himself up on one elbow. Jean was on the telephone, stooped over in the cone of light from a desk lamp.

'I can't speak louder, there's someone sleeping … No, it's not what you think. The past, nothing but the past. I'll tell you about it. What time did you say your plane was arriving on Wednesday? … Ten seventeen in the morning. I'll collect you … Did you find the catalogue at the Guggenheim Museum?'

Suddenly it was obvious to him. All that stood between Édouard and his new life was this alter ego, this ghostly double who was spluttering on the phone. By staring at him, he now saw Jean only as ectoplasm, a pallid shapeless form. There was no such thing as chance; matters were arranged with an implacable logic. Now he understood why Jean had led him here and why nature had made them both in the same mould. During dinner, Jean had, while speaking about his health, quoted a sentence: 'Death will catch me unawares, because I want it to.' Édouard grabbed the metal bird's feet and got up noiselessly. He was in his stocking feet, something Thérèse had seen to, no doubt.

'Three years since we last met? ... Possibly ... I don't notice. Time stands still here; nothing ever happens ... Excuse me a second ... Édouard?'

The bird's beak went a good ten centimetres into Jean's forehead. He had the same incredulous expression as Jean-Baptiste when the root had come away in his hands before he toppled into the void. The receiver fell to the floor, emitting 'Hello's like the cries of a rat. Édouard crushed it with his heel. Jean's arms flailed about in the air before he fell backwards, taking the armchair with him. The wading bird embedded in his skull seemed to be slaking its thirst on the dark blood running from the wound. Édouard seized the cigarette which was burning away in the ashtray and took a long drag. It tasted of dust. It didn't take long for Thérèse to appear.

'What's going on? Oh God!'

Hands clasped to her mouth, she fell to her knees in front of Jean's body, his legs still twitching convulsively. Édouard stood contemplating the scene reflected in the window. It was like one of those stupid depictions of the Descent from the Cross.

'What have you done?'

'It was suicide.'

'No! You've killed him. It's a crime!'

'Call it whatever you like.'

'You're insane! I'm calling the police.'

'The phone's not working.'

'But why? Why?'

'You couldn't understand. It's between him and me, a pact, an exchange. In any case he didn't have long to live.'

'But ... This isn't a natural death.'

'What does that mean, "natural death"? All deaths are natural or else it's death itself which isn't. Don't just stay there in front of that chair, shaking like a jelly! Do something ... well, I don't know what ... coffee, yes, make some coffee!'

Like an automaton she stood up and made her way to the kitchen. Édouard shrugged his shoulders. He was cold. As he went to fetch his jacket from the sofa he slipped on the pool of blood.

'Oh, it's disgusting! All that'll have to be cleaned up, do you hear me, Thérèse?'

The soil was loose at this spot in the garden, but despite all the strength in her arms it still took Thérèse almost two hours to dig a hole deep enough to lay Jean's body in.

'That should do, Thérèse. We'll bend him a little if needs be. Get out of there – it's almost dawn.'

Somehow or other they managed to bundle their host into his last resting place and, after covering him with earth, planted various flowers, taken from their pots, here and there on top to form an attractive flower bed.

'It's as pretty as a roundabout. All it needs now is an old wine press.'

'I can't think how you still have the heart to laugh. What are we going to do now?'

'Move in, of course. We were looking for a house, we've found it. You like it, don't you?'

'That's not the point. Sooner or later someone's going to worry about Jean's disappearance.'

'But Jean hasn't disappeared. He's right here in front of you.'

'You're not going to tell me that …'

'Yes! Didn't he benefit from our amazing twinhood for a

good part of my youth? It's my turn now. Believe me, I know him better than you do and he wouldn't hold this against me.'

'It's impossible!'

'No one's indispensable, you'll see. It's a second life I'm giving him. Put my jacket on, you'll catch a chill.'

The ribbons of mist were fraying on the tips of the pine trees. It was still too early to know whether it would be fine or not. What was certain was that a new day was dawning. A few skilful cuts from Thérèse's scissors and another man's face was appearing, with a towel knotted round his neck, in the bathroom mirror.

'The hair's fine but what about the moustache?'

'Let's say I shaved it off last night. It made me look old. Surely you're entitled to a change, aren't you? Or else I'll grow one.'

'And the scar?'

'A detail. Give me the razor.'

'Oh no!'

'Give me the razor and clear off!'

What pain was there to fear since this face was no longer his own? With no hesitation and a steady hand Édouard gashed his cheek and indeed felt nothing but a sort of leaking, the hissing of a punctured tyre. Alcohol on the wound had the effect of an invigorating slap like the one they give new babies to give them a taste of life. Once he'd put a sticking plaster on, Édouard smiled at himself in the mirror.

'Bloody Jean, indestructible!'

Jean's style of dress was sporty but understated, clothes in good taste and of good quality. They might have been made to measure for Édouard except for the shoes: in contrast to him, Jean's left foot was bigger than the right. He struck some poses like a toreador in front of the wardrobe mirror then, satisfied, joined Thérèse.

'What do you think then?'

'It's … It's truly amazing but …'

'But what?'

'The scar …'

'Yes?'

'You've got the wrong cheek.'

Mirrors are always playing tricks, but Édouard was unperturbed. Left, right, who would worry? For the moment other things were more pressing. They had to go to Geneva to retrieve their things from the hotel.

'Will you be able to drive this car?'

'It's an automatic; I don't know.'

'It's very simple: forward gear, reverse gear. Actually I should be able to manage it myself. Let me take the wheel.'

Thérèse wasn't entirely reassured but after a few kilometres she agreed that Édouard was acquitting himself very well. The gracefully negotiated bends followed one upon the other like the figures of an accomplished skater. The sun spread a gilded pollen in the air. There was a cassette in the car radio. Édouard pushed it in with the tip of his index finger. Berlioz's *Requiem* accompanied them in grand style right up to the Bristol.

Once the bill was paid and the luggage stowed in the boot,

Édouard and Thérèse found themselves burdened with a completely new freedom. It was half past ten and the weather was glorious.

'What do you say to a drive along the lake? We could have lunch in Thonon or Évian.'

'If you like.'

There was little traffic, camper vans in the main, driven by retired couples in no hurry to arrive anywhere. On the left a sign post announced 'EXCENEVEX, MEDIEVAL TOWN OF FLOWERS'.

'Tempted, Thérèse?'

'Why not?'

All the car parks charged a fee, which made Édouard lose his temper. So they parked some distance from the centre in a place where it was free, near a campsite where elderly people plastered in sun lotion were getting some fresh air outside their caravans. They found more of the same, only more suitably dressed, in the twisting narrow streets of the town. The women went into raptures over the window displays in the souvenir shops, while the men videoed the half-timbered balconies spewing torrents of geraniums. Every house was a business; everything was on sale: hand-knitted pullovers, sausages, cowbells, carved walking sticks, musical boxes shaped like chalets, handmade leather sandals, brightly coloured caps and T-shirts. The most unassuming little door claimed to be a '*crêperie*', a '*sandwicherie*', a '*friterie*' or an '*atelier d'art*'. The wrought-iron shop signs swung lazily in an asthmatic wind. As was proper, the visit to the town ended at the foot of a castle whose towers rose straight out of the lake. Happily there was no one at that spot. Thérèse and Édouard sat down on the flat polished stones which sloped down into the clear water. Ducks fluffed up their feathers, quacking. A woman dived off a yacht anchored a few metres out: 'Come on, Tony, it's lovely.' A silent aeroplane split the sky in two. In a room in the castle, someone was picking out notes on a piano, a clumsy approximation of a Chopin étude. Every sound ricocheted off the lake; the echo went on for ever. Thérèse seemed happy. Her gaze drifted over the smooth surface, far away, beyond the mountains in their turbans of wispy cloud.

'How peaceful it is ...'

'Let's go and look for a restaurant, but not in this madhouse.'

'Édouard?'

'Yes?'

'What about having a picnic?'

They went to the shops in Thonon. The streets were heaving with a multicoloured and very noisy crowd, halfway between a village festival and a riot. Édouard had left the choice of menu to Thérèse. He was waiting for her in front of the delicatessen with a baguette under his arm, in the company of an ageless poodle with watery eyes. Pennants of various colours were strung across the street, flapping in the wind, and loudspeakers crackled unintelligible announcements between salsa tracks. Certain places are non-places and Thonon-les-Bains was one of them. Édouard was convinced that if he were to go round behind the façades of the houses he would find only wooden stays, like the ones used to support scenery on a film set. Ditto with the people who, from the front, couldn't be more than one centimetre deep. In October they must fold all that up, leaving Thonon no more than a name on the map. That said, Geneva and Lyon had made the same impression on him. Doubtless because he was no longer in the cast list for this bad film and was glad of it. He had only one desire, to get the hell out of there. In a gap in the crowd, his attention was caught by the shopfront of an outdated clothes shop: 'A. CARON, founded 1887'. Diagonally across the window was a banner with 'EVERYTHING MUST GO' written in red on a white background. Behind the sign, two headless mannequins, one tall and slim, the other small and stout, sported identical beige and blue-sprigged dresses. The back of the shop was immersed in total darkness. Édouard couldn't help smiling when he recognised the two familiar figures, and touched his hat in greeting. Eventually Thérèse reappeared, hair all over the place, as if emerging from a gladiatorial combat.

'What a queue there was!'

'Let's get out of here.'

On their way out of the town, just past the Château Ripaille, they turned into a road at random. It led to the Gavot Plateau. The higher they climbed, the fewer houses there were and the easier it was to breathe. Just like locals, they went straight off along a little track lined with hazels which came out into an idyllic meadow argued over by sun and shadow. A wooden fence separated them from a field of piebald ponies, which ceased grazing to watch, wide-eyed, as the visitors sat down. After the bustle of the town, the infinitely peaceful sight of the animals charmed them. Édouard broke off a lump of bread and went over to the enclosure. A mare followed by her foal plodded over to meet him. Édouard stretched out his palm and stroked her nose. It felt hot and damp. A delicious smell of hay and leather was coming from her. The foal, like a bolster on top of two wobbly trestles, kept at a cautious distance. One by one the others came forward, as shy as they were intrigued. For a moment there was peace on earth, men, things and animals gathered together in the most perfect harmony. Édouard then made the mistake of throwing the piece of bread. Immediately the horses began fighting, biting one another and of course the strongest came out on top.

'Load of idiots …'

'Édouard, it's ready!'

Thérèse was radiant, like a celluloid doll appearing out of a fake cabbage. She looked as if she had fallen out of the sky, her blue dress spread out like a parachute on the green grass. The shadow of the leaves gave her a little veil.

'You look magnificent, just like a Watteau. So, what's on the menu?'

The ponies had gone back to their grazing, as indifferent to them as they were to the rest of creation. Thérèse was brushing some crumbs off her lap. Édouard was lying on his back, picking his teeth with a blade of grass.

'Édouard?'

'Yes?'

'What are you thinking about?'

'Nothing. I'm looking for the ogre.'

'Ogre?'

'The one in children's puzzles. "The ogre is hiding in the tree. Can you find him?"'

'Have you found him?'

'There are so many.'

'Doesn't this remind you of something?'

'What, the ogres?'

'No, here, now …'

'I give up.'

'The picnic at Nyons.'

'Oh yes, indeed.'

'How far away that seems, another life. I don't really know where I am any more. I have the feeling of going from dream to nightmare with nothing in between.'

'The best way to avoid getting lost is not to know where you're going. I read that somewhere – it's true.'

'But … Don't you feel any remorse?'

'No more than I feel regret. I'm alive and I'm sleepy.'

For some unknown reason the horses began to prance in the meadow, neighing. Édouard was already asleep, one arm covering his eyes. Thérèse stretched out next to him. A ladybird ventured onto her hand. 'Ladybird, will it be fine on Sunday?' The insect spread its glossy wings and flew away. It was Saturday.

It was quite beyond belief – how could strapping great lads like that flaunt themselves in that sort of outfit, striking poses that were downright ... Thérèse tried to find the appropriate adjective, then, having failed, shut the body-building magazine and put it back in the pile she'd taken it from. She knew that type of publication existed but she'd never had a look at one before. They didn't seem like Jean's sort of thing. Of course his slightly too fastidious manners, along with the place they had met him, left little doubt as to his tendencies, and she wasn't shocked. But 'that' was vulgar, just one step better than an advertisement for Boucherie Bernard. How can you tell with people? One side of the wall is always in the shade. She wondered what hers might be like, where her place in the shadow was and what vice might be lurking there. There were ten thousand or none at all. It was like when she was a little girl going to confession. She had been obliged to invent sins for herself, out of fear that if she had nothing to ask pardon for, people would suspect her of concealing horrors. Hatred and jealousy were foreign to her; she had never envied anybody anything, nor harmed anyone. She didn't consider herself a saint but it had to be admitted that the sum of her sins would not weigh very heavily in the scales at the Last Judgement. She wasn't proud of this, merely astonished. In this respect she wasn't exactly like everyone else, and had sometimes suffered for it, as if it were a sort of character flaw. That said, she was still complicit in a murder. Two days before, she'd been digging a grave in the dead of night and burying the body of a man she'd known for only a few hours. She was aware of this, without managing entirely to believe it. Life had resumed its course, as peaceful and serene as at Rémuzat before Jean-Baptiste's arrival. Only the scenery had changed; eagles had replaced vultures. It was nice on the balcony; it smelled of wood and hot pine resin.

'Well, Thérèse, getting a tan? Here's the mail – I ran into the postman.'

'The postman?'

'At the end of the track. It was "Bonjour, M'sieur Marissal. Lovely weather!" We talked about this and that. He's a very pleasant young man.'

'He didn't …'

'Not for one second. Let's see … Bank statement … advert … advert … and a body-building magazine. Nothing very interesting.'

'It's not right to open his mail.'

'Why not? He's got nothing to hide any more, neither the state of his bank account – which, by the way, seems satisfactory – nor his little foibles. And stop talking about him; you'll give me a split personality. I'm Jean Marissal and I'm even going to start painting again.'

'You?'

'Of course. At the end of his life Monet was painting with two stumps, and I've still got one good arm. The studio's never been used – there's not a spot of paint, nor the slightest whiff of turpentine. That poor Jean's latest canvases are painful to look at. Nothing but portraits of children – star pupils, not a hair out of place, absolutely perfect in their execution but quite devoid of emotion. An orphans' gallery! I can see why he stopped doing it altogether. Have you seen them?'

'No, I've not been downstairs.'

'Good God, Thérèse, own the place, fill the space. Get out of your kitchen and your laundry room, broaden your horizons!'

'I will, I'll go. What do you want for lunch?'

Édouard wondered which annoyed him more, the strands of air-dried beef stuck between two of his teeth or Thérèse's extraordinarily apathetic reaction to their new situation. What would it take before the umbilical cord keeping her on a leash from the larder to the balcony, from the balcony to the laundry, broke? Enough had happened since he'd taken her on: a son gobbled up by vultures, a significant inheritance, a brand-new wardrobe, a Swiss chalet rid of its owner … Damn it! What was wrong with the fat cow? But no, even on tiptoe a dwarf is still a dwarf.

The tiny bit of meat exploded onto the balcony rail, as if shot out through a pea-shooter. Thérèse was sleeping peacefully, mouth half open, snoring gently, her chubby hands with their palms like cats' pads turned up to the sky on the lounger's armrests, her legs stretched out, feet turned inwards … 'Fat cow,' he repeated through clenched teeth, but with all the candour of a child encountering a fat cow for the first time.

As he got up from the wicker chair he could not have said which of them creaked more. The sky was paved with clouds; there was no one up there any more. The great puppetmaster had let go of the strings. Even the trees were sagging.

The big empty room frightened him. The silence especially, nibbled by the mandibles of unidentifiable insects. In Switzerland time seems slow but it's just an illusion. An implacable stopwatch has it on a leash and every last second is counted, stored, recorded. There nothing is left to chance because chance has been bought as well. No risks are taken. Lake Geneva will never flood.

Édouard sat down behind the desk, drummed his fingers on the green morocco-leather blotter and began opening the drawers. The first held nothing but boring paperwork – receipts, insurance policies, chequebooks – all of it in a total mess. Clearly Jean was no longer keeping on top of things, just letting them pile up. Most of the envelopes hadn't even been opened. The second contained a small nickel-plated 6.35-calibre revolver with a mother-of-pearl handle, and a dozen unremarkable photos, taken in Morocco no doubt – palm groves, ochre mud buildings, red sand dunes. Jean figured only in the last one, along with a tanned young blonde girl who was smiling broadly into the lens. She had her arm round Jean's waist and was resting her head on his shoulder. His arms were folded across his chest, and he stood stiff as a post, screwing up his eyes, grimacing. They seemed to be in the middle of nowhere, white ground and uniformly blue sky. The desert perhaps? The print had been torn and stuck together again with sticky tape. It must go back a number of years. Jean didn't yet have the look of a dead man. The third drawer was locked. Édouard forced it, using a paperknife in the shape of a salamander with the blade as its tail. Strangely all he found there was a bent paper clip. Evidently Jean had had a clear-out and wiped the slate clean where his past was concerned. Apart from Édouard's visit, he could no longer have been expecting much from life and had left the place in the state in which he had found it on moving in. Édouard was grateful for his consideration, which allowed him to assume Jean's identity without burdening himself with his memory. He then spent a good hour imitating his signature for no particular reason, the way you kill time in the dentist's waiting room by doing a crossword.

Thérèse woke up lying sideways, with sunburn on her left cheek. She had never in her life been drunk but this siesta gave her a vague idea of what a hangover might be like. It was because of that stupid dream in which she and Édouard were flushing eagles out of burrows, a dark labyrinth which smelled of soil and hen droppings. They were moving around on all fours, their mouths and nostrils full of feathers, their hands and knees crushing eggs which groaned. Édouard was going ahead of her like a furious mole: 'And another one!' Dreams were stupid, so stupid that you ended up believing them.

With furred-up mouth, unsteady on her feet, she took refuge in the kitchen and swallowed two big glasses of water one after the other. The clock said five. It was still too early to start cooking but she needed to occupy her hands in order to rid herself of her head. Not much was left in the fridge or cupboards – a few potatoes, some shallots, a pack of smoked herring. She plunged the potatoes into a pan of salted water, staring at it until it came to the boil. Then she chopped the shallots as finely as possible to make it take longer. As long as her hands were doing something, nothing could happen to her. What little good sense she still had lived in her ten reddened fingers with their broken nails. She didn't want to think about anything any more, anything at all. If Édouard had arrived unexpectedly she could have stuck the vegetable peeler into his throat without batting an eyelid. Frightened by this sudden upsurge of violence, she let go of the knife and collapsed onto a chair, arms hanging by her sides. 'I'm going mad as well now ...'

During his school days Édouard had many a time used his talents as a forger to get his schoolmates out of a jam – school reports, absence notes – always in return for a reward of course. Jean himself had called on his services. By now Édouard could imitate his signature with his eyes closed – a merely stylistic exercise, because in no way was he thinking of emptying the dead man's bank account. What would he have done with it? He was richer than him. It was a way of putting himself in the character's skin, unless it was the other way round … Let's just say that they were currently proceeding hand in hand. He crumpled up the scribbled pages and threw them into the wastepaper basket. It was as he was straightening up again that his eye fell on the little silver box Jean had sniffed the powder from on their first evening. He opened it, licked the tip of his finger and tasted it. It was bitter, like all medicines. Closing it again, he automatically pocketed it before going downstairs to the studio.

As the house was built on the side of a hill, the studio, like the ground floor, benefited from a large picture window through which light poured in. An armchair, a sofa, a large Godin stove and an enormous studio easel that was like some medieval instrument of torture made up the furniture.

Édouard pulled out one of the dozen canvases stacked with their faces to the wall, and placed it on the easel. It depicted someone near life-size, a young woman or a young man, you couldn't really tell, seen from behind, head turned, appearing to look over their shoulder. Édouard uncorked a bottle of turpentine and soaked a rag in it. At school he had always volunteered to clean the blackboard. Verb tables, divisions, multiplications, date and moral for the day would disappear as he wiped, and soon there remained on the black surface only a tangle of large figures of eight, dripping with milky water which dried in patches. Yesterday turned into tomorrow, a single day always starting afresh, eternity in the everyday. His arm had instinctively rediscovered this windscreen-wiper movement and little by little the adolescent face disappeared, making way for a strange landscape in which the colours ran together according to the fickle rules of chance. Édouard was triumphant, intoxicated by the solvent fumes and the certainty of having opened the door which had been shut in Jean's face.

'Form is limitation, poor old Jean, form is imitation! Vanity, nothing more! Outlines are confines, the sky has no angles! The body is unstable, that's why it's survived!'

Gripped by a frenzy worthy of Bernard Palissy burning his furniture as his wife looked on in terror, Édouard gave three or four other paintings the same treatment, before Thérèse arrived.

'What are you doing, all covered in paint? You're behaving like a madman!'

'Look, Thérèse, look! That's astonished you, eh?'

'That doesn't look like anything, all those daubings.'

'Exactly! Exactly.'

'You really have no respect for anything ...'

'But you don't understand. It's the opposite – I'm carrying on his work, going where he was never able to go because he was so trammelled by his knowledge ... I'm un-teaching him, that's it ... Un-teaching him!'

'Lovely paintings like that ... Right, go and wash your hands, it's ready.'

Thérèse's reaction in no way dented Édouard's morale. A good many artists before him had suffered the incomprehension of those around them. However, as he sat down to eat he reproached her for not cooking him something hot.

'Don't you like my herring salad?'

'I do, but I'd have preferred soup, a nice soup. You make such good ones.'

'For that I'd need something to make it with. There's nothing here but tinned food.'

'Tomorrow we'll go shopping. Speaking of which, what day is it?'

'Tuesday.'

'Then tomorrow's Wednesday ... Wednesday ... We've nothing planned for Wednesday?'

'What would we have planned?'

'I don't know ... It seemed to me ... Pah ... I'd like a little more please, I'm as hungry as a wolf. What's wrong now,

Thérèse? You've got ever such a long face.'

'I can't do it!'

'Do what?'

'Get used to the idea that we're murderers!'

She collapsed sobbing on the edge of the table. Édouard was stunned. It was all so simple, so obvious ...

'Come now, Thérèse, my dear ...'

He stood up and took her in his arms, gently patting her on the shoulder.

'You're too emotional. Give yourself up to the great happiness we've been given.'

She put her arms round his waist, her head nestling against his stomach.

'If that were true, there's nothing I'd like better ... Why did you do it?'

'You don't get something for nothing.'

'But you're not short of money – we could have rented a house.'

'This was the one, there wasn't any other one. I knew it as soon as I set foot here. And Jean knew that too.'

'What would you know about that?'

'I know because I am him. Now stop your moaning, enter into the game and play your part, for goodness' sake. You'll never have a better one. Stop looking over your shoulder, there's no one following you. You're like me and Jean, you have no past. Who's going to weep for us? You're giving us too much importance.'

*

The night was pitch-dark, an immense sky, like a cavern. Billions of stars speckled the picture window, indifferent to the unaccustomed sight of a hysterical old man daubing solvent onto warped canvases in the company of a woman flat out on a sofa, both of them bathed in a jelly of white light.

'You see, Thérèse, literature wasn't made for me – too complicated, too ambiguous, too many words, mere soap bubbles! Whereas painting, it's concrete, material, sensual, real! Am I right?'

Thérèse had no opinion on the subject, nor on any other. She was floating, her whole being absorbed by the supreme power of the white powder which Édouard had made her sniff.

'What is it?'

'A medicine. It's very good for what you've got. Close one nostril and breathe in very deeply.'

'Is this a drug?'

'Go on, for heaven's sake.'

Thérèse wasn't fooled but had succumbed to the powerful need to rid herself at all costs of the anguish which held her captive. It was like an atomic mushroom exploding in her head, an orgasm which sent her off into unimaginable spheres from which she descended gently, as if with the aid of a parachute, to land, ecstatic, on this sofa as soft as a cushion filled with rose petals. She had administered morphine to terminally ill patients in the final stages and now she recalled how their faces were transformed, the pain slipping away, forming a kind of halo … Now she understood. Death was nothing, nor was life … But survival! Édouard had taken some as well but the product didn't have the same effect on him … He was gesticulating non-stop, arguing with himself as he rubbed the solvent-soaked rag over Jean's canvases and, she had to admit, allowed much richer forms and colours to come through than those originally depicted by the painting.

'Making a white rabbit come out of a hat, that's a conjuring trick; anyone can do that, but drawing a hat out of a white rabbit, that's real magic! Do you grasp the distinction, Thérèse?'

Thérèse couldn't have cared less. Her eyelids were growing heavy and she felt better than ever. The persistent smell of petrol proved that paradise was nothing but a huge garage, and on this certainty she sank voluptuously into the most perfect no man's land.

Édouard had taken hold of another canvas, which showed a young Adonis reclining at the foot of an oak tree. The rag went to work again but unlike the other paintings the bland image was hiding another: two ladies, standing, identically clothed in the same pale dress with a blue pattern, the smaller afflicted by a divergent squint and the other straight as a letter i with its dot disappearing under a vault of shade. Édouard burst out laughing: 'You're indefatigable! I wish you good evening, Mesdames. Make yourselves at home.'

Édouard could have slept for no more than a couple of hours yet he felt on top form, fresh as a daisy, with such an appetite for life. Thérèse was still sleeping, rolled up in a cocoon of sheets and covers.

'Well now, Thérèse, wake up! It's almost ten o'clock. We've got shopping to do.'

On automatic pilot she took her shower, swallowed a bowl of coffee and, without knowing quite how, found herself at the steering wheel.

'I'm driving?'

'You've got to start. Imagine if something were to happen to me. I may be immortal but no one is proof against a bad cold. It's child's play, you'll see.'

And indeed, despite swerving a few times starting off, Thérèse soon felt as much at ease as on the sofa where she had spent the evening. She was not to exceed 60 kmh. The effects of the drug she'd taken the evening before were still there and her head lurched this way and that like a jar full of a thick, sweet liquid.

'How are you feeling?'

'Well, very well … A little woozy. But fine.'

'That stuff's amazing, isn't it?'

'Yes.'

'No wonder young people take drugs.'

They burst out laughing like a couple of kids hiding behind a curtain.

They made some random purchases in the village minimarket, where Monsieur Marissal was greeted very deferentially, which sent them into a new fit of uncontrollable giggles. Nothing was real, everything was allowed. On the way back they listened to the radio news. A footballer had just been bought by a club for some incredible sum, and a husband and father, unemployed and crippled with debt, had just wiped out his family before killing himself in a bungalow in the Pas-de-Calais region. A storm was expected in the evening, and traffic jams on roads out of Lyon. It was a perfect world.

Someone was waiting for them outside the door, a tall blonde girl who rushed towards them as soon as they had parked.

'Where have you been, Papa? You were supposed to collect me from the airport.'

Like two insects in amber, Thérèse and Édouard stared dumbstruck at the bizarre apparition framed by the car window. The girl must have been twenty-five or thirty years old, with clear skin and glossy hair, not unattractive, although her teeth seemed slightly too big for her mouth. Her features vaguely reminded Édouard of someone.

'I tried to call you but your phone's out of order.'

Édouard drew his hand over his face like an actor pulling on his mask. The girl, good God, the girl! In a split second he identified her: she was the one in the photo which had been torn and stuck together again, now a few years older.

'I'm sorry, my dear, I completely forgot. I worked all night. Have you been waiting long?'

'The taxi dropped me off half an hour ago. I was beginning to worry …'

'I'm really sorry … Thérèse, let me introduce my daughter …'

166

The young woman got him out of an awkward situation by introducing herself, offering her hand through the window.

'Sharon.'

'Delighted to meet you. Go ahead, Monsieur Jean, I'll see to the shopping.'

Édouard dragged himself from the car and let himself be kissed on both cheeks.

'Have you shaved your moustache off? It makes you look younger. You seem on top form. So this is where you live? It's magnificent but, my God, it's isolated! The taxi driver had a hell of a time finding it. "Low Heights", what a funny name.'

'Did you have a good journey?'

'I almost missed the plane in New York thanks to Gladys. In the space of a week I only ever saw her in passing, then at the last moment she remembered I was there. But you know her …'

'Of course, yes.'

Édouard was getting flustered with the lock. He couldn't find the right key among the bunch.

'What's wrong with your arm? Have you hurt it?'

'Nothing. No, I … I had a stroke a few months ago. Paralysis of the left side. Everything's fine now except for this arm.'

'Why didn't you say anything?'

'Old people's stuff, no one's interested. I can manage, I tell you. There, go in.'

Immediately they were inside, a furious desire to shove

the girl into the cupboard under the stairs and double-lock the bolt came into his head. CLICK CLACK! Jean's offspring out of the way; out of sight, out of mind the girl with the big teeth – good riddance! But she was already making her way into the sitting room.

'Lovely space! You must feel lost, all alone in here?'

'I'm not alone.'

'True. And who is Thérèse?'

'My nurse. To begin with I couldn't do much on my own. She still helps me a lot. Plus she's excellent company.'

'It's still strange for me to see you with a woman.'

'There was your mother, you know!'

'Gladys isn't a mother or a woman, you know that as well as I do.'

'Yes, all right. Do you want me to show you to your room? You'd no doubt like to freshen up.'

'I would, yes.'

In the kitchen Thérèse was weeping hot tears over a heap of thinly sliced onions.

'What are you making?'

'Gratinée à l'oignon. You wanted soup so I'm making soup.'

'But … that's a very good idea.'

'What is she doing?'

'Taking a shower.'

'I told you this would end badly.'

The blade of the knife rammed into the chopping board vibrated like a tuning fork. The tears reddening Thérèse's eyes were not just from peeling onions. Édouard shrugged his shoulders, fiddling with a packet of grated Gruyère.

'I can't help it if I've got a big family.'

Sharon gave the plastic shower curtain a sharp tug, heart pounding. Of course there was no old woman hiding behind it, brandishing a butcher's knife. She stuck her tongue out at her reflection in the mirror and rubbed herself vigorously, without, however, being able to banish the strange unease which had gripped her since she'd been reunited with her father. It was stupid but she didn't recognise him. It was him and yet not him. It wasn't to do with the absence of his moustache any more than with his disability, nor the fact that she hadn't seen him for almost three years. It was something else – the stiff, staccato way he moved and his voice which crunched words like glass. Maybe the stroke had changed him … But when it came down to it, how well did she really know him anyway? In twenty-seven years of existence she had crossed paths with him only five or six times. Until she was eighteen Gladys had let her believe that he was dead. If it hadn't been for that fortuitous encounter at a private view at a New York gallery she would never have suspected his existence. He had been as surprised as she was since her bitch of a mother had never informed him of her birth. One month later, free of her mother's authority, she joined him in Morocco where he was living at that time. He hadn't been against her coming and had shown himself full of goodwill and consideration towards her, but she had quickly understood that there was no place for an eighteen-year-old girl in the life he was leading. The drugs and the young boys took up too much space. She hadn't resented him for it and had led her own life, while staying in regular contact with him by post or telephone, or by meeting up with him here or there, in London, Paris or Berlin, wherever fate brought them together. They had never spent more than four or five days together, just enough time to share superficial pleasures and take leave of each other awkwardly on a station platform or in an airport waiting area. Their relationship was difficult to define. Love had never had time to blossom but the sporadic meetings had ended up creating a tender complicity between them as if they shared a secret, though neither of them knew what that secret was. Perhaps it was just an irrepressible attraction to the void? She had known he was ill for several years, which was why he had left Morocco for Switzerland, but this stroke did not tally with the usual symptoms of the virus he had. Apart from the bent arm he appeared to be in perfect health. If that hag Gladys had not refused her the five thousand dollars she needed to open her interior design studio she would never have made the journey here, such was her fear of illness and death. Only the lease had to be signed in two days' time and this was her only option.

Having blasted her hair dry until she had restored its full bounce, she put on a T-shirt, a clean pair of jeans and some trainers and left her room, sticking her chest out like a boxer making for the ring.

Édouard was waiting for her on the balcony, a cardigan over his shoulders, at a low table with several bottles of alcohol lined up on it. He seemed older than he had just before.

'Here, the Guggenheim catalogue you asked me to get.'

'Thank you, Sharon. What will you have?'

'The usual.'

Édouard hesitated. There was Scotch, vodka and white Martini. He reached for the last.

'With an olive.'

'Of course, I haven't forgotten.'

He served her and began leafing through the catalogue.

'You've started working again then? From what you'd told me, I thought there was no question of that.'

'Let's call it a relapse.'

'Will you show me?'

'If you like, but it's still at the sketch stage. To you then!'

'To us! … What, are you drinking whisky now?'

'At my age you can't taste anything or else you like everything, which comes to the same thing.'

The clink of ice cubes answered the rumbling of the storm which was announcing its arrival by sending thick clouds scudding over the lake.

'Isn't Thérèse joining us for a drink?'

'She's coming. She's a little shy. We live like bears in a cave here. Do you like onion soup?'

'I'll never forget the one we ate together the last time we saw each other, at the Pied du Cochon in Les Halles in Paris. Do you remember?'

'Of course, what an evening!'

A blast of infernal heat made Thérèse take a step backwards when she opened the oven door. The layer of golden Gruyère was rising, letting out little jets of steam, each bowl like a mini volcano. On the table the apple and walnut salad sat alongside the cheese platter. All that was missing was the guests. Thérèse wiped her eyes with a corner of her apron, a ridiculous apron made to look like the torso of a woman wearing a bra and sexy knickers. There weren't any others. Thérèse could put off no longer the inevitable confrontation with the girl who had appeared from goodness knows where. She wasn't the one from whom a blunder was to be feared, because after all she wasn't supposed to know of Sharon's existence, but rather it was Édouard. The high-wire act on which he had embarked, without even the flimsiest safety net, was making her panic. He reminded her of the tarot card, the Fool, depicting a vagabond with his head in the air and a meagre bundle on his shoulder, one foot poised over a void, and a dog hanging on his coat-tails. No matter how crafty or diabolically cool-headed he was, some day or other he would end up falling into the void, and this girl, this Sharon, was the void. That was visible in her excessively blue eyes, like two small bottomless lakes. For the first time in her life she felt hatred towards someone and was horrified by this. She jumped as if she'd been caught in the act of an evil thought when Édouard called her.

'Aren't you joining us for a drink, Thérèse?'

'No, thank you.'

'So it's ready, is it? Can we eat?'

'Er ... yes.'

The soup was scalding but delicious accompanied by an excellent white wine of which Édouard, to Thérèse's relief, partook in moderation. Contrary to her fears he was behaving like a worthy patriarch, sober and sparing in his words. As Thérèse was no more talkative than Édouard, the responsibility of making conversation fell on Sharon. Once the anecdotes about the crazy life people led in New York and treacherous attacks on a certain Gladys, her mother, were over, they learned that Sharon had been living in Munich for five years and was counting on opening an interior design studio there in the near future, with someone called Monica.

'Like I told you on the phone the other day, I've brought the file. You'll see, it's a gold mine! But we can talk about that later, can't we?'

'Whenever you like.'

Then, as nothing could top that, the conversation lapsed into more anodyne subjects like the weather forecast, the swift passage of time, the peaceful beauty of the Swiss landscape and, finally, the recipe for the onion soup. By coffee, absolute silence reigned over the cups and Édouard almost knocked his over by nodding off at the table.

'You'll have to forgive me, I need to rest for a little while. Wake me in an hour, Thérèse.'

'Of course, Éd— Monsieur Jean.'

To hide the confusion which was making her blush, Thérèse began clearing the table. Sharon did not appear to have noticed her slip. She was inspecting her chewed nails with a look of disgust.

'I've tried everything – lacquer, medication, therapy. I can't do anything about it; it's been like this ever since I was tiny.'

'You must have an anxious nature.'

'That's for sure. I wonder whether I get that from my mother or my father ... While we're on the subject, Thérèse, how do you think my father is?'

'But ... well. He's made a very good recovery. It's not out of the question that he might regain the use of his arm some day.'

'I didn't mean physically. Still, I have to admit I'm amazed to see him in such good health. AIDS doesn't usually regress like that.'

'AIDS?'

'You do know my father's HIV positive?'

'Yes, of course ... But Monsieur Jean is someone of great courage, a real fighter.'

'That must have happened late in the day. The last time I spoke to him on the phone he seemed, well, resigned.'

'He has his ups and downs like everyone else.'

'No doubt. But even before he was ill I never saw him look like that, fierce, authoritarian. I don't know whether to be glad about it or frightened. It's as if he were possessed.'

'By who?'

'I don't know.'

'He's seriously ill; seriously ill people are always unpredictable.'

'Yes, I'm sure you're right. You know more about it than me. How long have you worked for him?'

'Nearly a year.'

'A year! Why has he never said anything to me about you?'

'I suppose he didn't want to worry you.'

'And he's never spoken about me to you?'

'Not in so many words. He's a very private man.'

'Very! But I'm bothering you with all my questions. I'm sorry, Thérèse, it's because I'm concerned about him.'

'That's only natural.'

'I think I'll have a short rest as well. See you later.'

Jean had AIDS! Of course, with the life he led, that emaciated body, the thin hair and the whole heap of medicines in the bathroom. Why hadn't Thérèse thought of it earlier? But she had never mixed with that kind of people. For her it was a young person's disease … And she didn't know any young people. She knew next to nothing about the disease, only what she'd heard on the TV and radio … Leprosy, the Black Death, she could have coped with them, but AIDS? How was she going to be able to answer Sharon's questions? Once she had rinsed the sink, Thérèse took off her rubber gloves and looked at her hands. They were redder perhaps than the young woman's, but in a better state. If her own nails were short it was because she cut them regularly every week for reasons of cleanliness. She had never bitten them, even at the most anxious moments of her life. She'd broken some, of course she had, scrubbing other people's toilets or scouring the bottoms of their saucepans, but she had never bitten them. They were strong, hard as horn. A pretty girl like that with such ugly hands, she must have been through some really tough times! She wasn't a bad kid, even if she did give herself airs, a little girl who'd put on her mother's high heels, that was all … The concern she showed for her father was touching … touching but really annoying.

Thérèse gripped the edge of the sink with both hands as if she wanted to pull it off.

'Oh, Édouard, lies are so complicated!'

The house whistled like an ageing lung. Outside, the wind prowled in search of cracks and already raindrops were splattering onto the picture window. Sharon had never liked mountains; they made her feel like listening to Wagner and she loathed Wagner. She disliked the house too, unless it was the other way round. All the empty, silent space was crushing her.

There was nothing in the desk drawers, nothing of interest except for the photo of herself and her father, torn and stuck together again, and a small women's pistol which she had put in her pocket after discovering in the wastepaper basket three crumpled pages covered in her father's signature, going progressively from the clumsiest to the most assured.

'Who are these people?'

The photo trembled in her hand. The rip was vertical as if someone had wanted to separate the two figures. Sharon had just turned eighteen and she was meeting her father for the second time. The snap had been taken the day after she arrived on the beach at Essaouira. A powerful wind was whipping up the sand, stinging her arms and legs like buckshot. As she huddled against her father for protection she had felt him stiffen. He said, 'I'm sorry,' in a strangled voice, the way people do when they bump into someone on the train. It had been Omar holding the camera, the son of the people who were renting the house to her father. She had been in love with him for the week of her visit. Unfortunately Omar preferred her father.

Sharon closed her eyes. Who was this man who was passing himself off as him? It was clear: in the photo the scar ran down the other cheek. It wasn't really fear that she felt, but a sort of stage fright. She found herself in the position of an actor who had been put on stage at the end of a play without knowing its denouement. No doubt she had a part to play in it, but which one? Murderer or victim?

It wouldn't be long now. The sky was chewing iron, sharpening its lightning bolts on the peaks of the mountains.

'Let it out, let it all out.'

At last his bladder let go and blissfully, eyes half closed, Édouard relieved himself before noticing, as he did up his flies, that he'd urinated on his wardrobe.

'Oh shit! Well, if people keep changing the layout of the rooms all the time without telling me!'

Whose fault was it? Huh? Whose fault? That slattern Thérèse's, of course! You couldn't rely on her. Oh, she was very good at daydreaming in the kitchen. But when it came to informing him the toilet had been moved, she was useless! Useless! In any case, he didn't need anyone any more; he'd give her notice tomorrow and good riddance! Because he had work to do – he wasn't just an extra on this earth, he had a task to accomplish, something brilliant that had come to him in his sleep: the essence, get back to the essence of things … His previous night's work was just a preliminary; he had to rub, keep rubbing, right down to the canvas and beyond! And next … He could no longer remember but there was a next, he was sure of that …

He put on his yellow shoes without tying the laces and almost fell flat on his face on the staircase.

'Are you going through my drawers?'

'Oh, you're awake now? I was looking at our photo.'

'Which photo?'

'This one, at Essaouira.'

'Oh yes. You haven't changed.'

'You have.'

'That's because old people age more quickly than young ones. That's nature, you can't do anything about it. I'm sorry, but I've got work … What's got into you?'

Sharon was aiming the little 6.35 at him.

'Who are you?'

'What d'you mean, who am I? Your damn fool of a father, that's who!'

Édouard and Sharon both jumped at the same moment. The lightning must have struck not far off. Édouard was the first to regain his composure.

'How much do you need?'

'You're not my father!'

'But what makes you think that?'

'The scar on your cheek, the three pages of practice signatures … And then your tone, your expression, the way you move, that energy! My father had AIDS, he was worn out. Damn it, I am his daughter, after all.'

'Oh, here we go, blood ties, family feeling, all nonsense. Enough, let's get this over with. You've come to get money out of me, that's the sole reason for your visit. Well, forget about the violins, how much do you want?'

'What have you done with him?'

'Aargh, she's so annoying! All right then, he is dead, dead and buried. How much? You can double it.'

It was almost dark. Sharon put on the desk lamp. The pistol appeared fake in her hand, as harmless as a cigarette lighter. With her other hand she took a mobile phone out of her pocket.

'I'm calling the police.'

'We'll see. Do you think that thing's going to work round here in weather like this? He's dead, I tell you, stiff as a board and eaten by worms by now, like any self-respecting

Christian. You've arrived too late, I'm afraid, but I can take his place very advantageously.'

'You killed him for his money?'

Édouard burst out laughing, slapping his thigh, and yet he didn't want to. Big Teeth was beginning to seriously rattle him He was going to squash her with the back of his hand like a gnat.

'Oh, my poor dear, I'm much richer than him. Go on, put that … thing down and we'll talk business. I'll leave you all his possessions and add half as much again for emotional collateral damage. How's that?'

'I don't know who you are but one thing I'm sure about is that you're utterly mad.'

'But your father was mad too. I knew him better than you did and for much longer. One father or another, for what you need him for, we won't quibble …'

'Murderer! I'm calling the police.'

They both screwed up their eyes as if looking into the flash in a photo booth. The lightning stopped time for just long enough to see Thérèse brandishing the bronze stork over Sharon's head.

'No! Don't do that, Thérèse!'

Édouard stretched out his arm, his hand open.

A gunshot rang out and Thérèse's menacing form vanished at the same time as the room sank into total darkness.

'The light, for God's sake, the light!'

Sharon's presence was evident now only from a poodle-like panting, which was answered by Thérèse's moans.

'Put the light on, damn it!'

'The power's gone.'

Édouard lit his cigarette lighter and got down on all fours beside Thérèse. She was lying on her back, eyes wide open, pink blood frothing at the corners of her mouth. The lighter flame was burning his fingers. He had to keep relighting it.

'There's a candle on the desk. Quick, give it to me!'

In the light from the flame, Thérèse appeared to be smiling: 'You were right, Édouard. It's not really that terrible … It happens so fast … I thought I was doing the right thing. I'm sorry about Sharon. I know you can't hear me, that my heart has stopped beating, that I'm dead. But I have no regrets, Édouard. I loved you, very much …'

'Is … is she dead?'

Édouard stood up, his face blank, devoid of all expression.

'When you shoot someone at point-blank range you have to envisage this kind of eventuality. You have just killed the most innocent of creatures.'

'But she was threatening me. It was self-defence!'

'Oh please … This isn't the moment. Keep it for your lawyer and your judges. And put that gun down; you've done enough, don't you think?'

'No, you're going to kill me.'

'Are you completely stupid or something? What would I do with your body? I need your arms. There's a spade in the shed. They may not have known each other long but Thérèse and Jean seemed to get along well.'

'You're useless! Your omelette's foul. Thérèse had her faults but she never ruined an omelette. Besides, you're clumsy with everything. You managed to decapitate your father when you were digging the hole for Thérèse.'

'You're vile!'

'No. I like work done well. I've always been demanding with my employees, firm but fair.'

'I'm not your employee!'

'As good as. The choice is yours. Either I sign everything you want, the money's yours, and you can set up wherever you want, or we both get dragged into sordid legal proceedings. I would remind you that you have your whole life ahead of you and where I'm concerned my past has no future. Do you understand? I'll give you two hours to think about all that. The clock's ticking and your mobile is in your pocket. See you later.'

Édouard wasn't sleepy. It was nice walking among the pine trees. A subtle smell of mushrooms was coming from the undergrowth. A quilt of white mist still covered the lake. Édouard sat down on a rock. A bright-orange slug was nonchalantly moving among the bedewed blades of grass.

'You should have let me sort this business out on my own, Thérèse. I'd soon have got that kid to change her tune. I shall miss you. I already miss you.'

Sharon's bag was waiting in the hallway like an overweight dog. The taxi would be there any minute.

'You're really going to stay here?'

'Of course. I like it here. I liked it the moment I set foot in the place. This is my home. It's different for you, and it would be best if we never saw each other again. A regular cheque as we agreed, but nothing else.'

'Don't worry, I've no intention of coming back here.'

'Then all's well. Ah, there's your car.'

The Mercedes bumped along the track and drew up in front of them. The driver, a small stocky man with an exotic accent, greeted them and stowed the luggage in the boot while Édouard took Sharon in his arms.

'See you soon, my dear, take good care of yourself.'

'Murderer.'

'You too, you too …'

The car turned round and disappeared behind the trees. Édouard rubbed his aching back and went to glance over the flower bed. Rhododendrons, maybe, or canna lilies? That would look classy …

'Hello?'

'Monsieur Marissal?'

'Speaking.'

'I'm ringing about the advertisement, the live-in nurse.'

'Yes.'

'Well, I'm interested in it.'

'Do you have references?'

'Of course.'

'How old are you?'

'Forty-five.'

'That's very young.'

'Do you think so? Generally people find the opposite, that ...'

'It's not important. Aside from your professional skills can you cook, look after a house?'

'Certainly. I've already ...'

'And gardening?'

'I love the countryside; I spent my entire youth there.'

'The location is quite ... austere.'

'That doesn't frighten me. I don't like cities.'

'You know my conditions, no visits, one day off per week and ...'

'I know about them, they're fine and so is the salary.'

'What's your name?'

'Carmen.'

'You're Spanish?'

'No. My father loved opera.'

'When can you start?'

'Tomorrow.'

'Good, take a taxi. I'll expect you at eleven o'clock. Be on time, I hate waiting.'

'You can count on me. See you tomorrow, then. Goodbye.'

'See you tomorrow.'

Carmen, what a name! She'll be called Thérèse and that's that.

Then he went to make too generous a lunch, as if he were expecting a visit. From two ladies passing by, perhaps?